*Justine,*

*Thanks a*
*appreciated :)*

# NO REST
# FOR THE
# WICKED

DANE COBAIN

## FORSAKEN
Seattle, WA 2015

Cover Design by Ashley Ruggirello
Edited by Laura Bartha

*This is a work of fiction. Names, characters, places, brands, media, and incidents are either the product of the author's imagination or are used fictitiously. Any resemblance to similarly named places or to persons living or deceased is unintentional.*

PRINT ISBN 978-1-62015-902-6
EPUB ISBN 978-1-62015-933-0
Library of Congress Control Number: 2015907227

# CHAPTER ONE: A FAIR TRIAL

*Wednesday November 11th, 2009*

**THEY GREW** out of the darkness, mysterious shapes hiding in plain sight in abstract mockery of the senses.

In the living room of a dingy flat in Hammersmith, tall and proud and shimmering in the air like a mirage, they stood; the only other light was a flickering television set that broadcast white noise to the sleeping occupant of the sofa.

"Wake."

Their shared voice echoed around the room like an organ in a cathedral, as powerful as independent thought. None of them moved – they just quaked with anticipation. The heap of dirty clothes on the sofa began to move and an ashen face emerged. He looked around the room in a sleepy daze. A matted beard framed his sunken eyes – grey on grey. He smelled like a pub before the smoking ban – an unpleasant cologne of nicotine and whiskey. When he saw that he wasn't alone, he climbed unsteadily to his feet.

"Who are you?" he asked, shading his eyes to look at them. "What are you doing in my house?" With every passing second, his eyes adjusted and grew wider.

"Our identity is unimportant." Their voices echoed around the room in perfect harmony, the eerie unison astounding, incredible, and terrifying. "We are defined by our purpose. You should already know what we are."

"Angels," he replied, avoiding their ferocious stare. "I've heard of you. But you're not real."

"Are you?" they asked, and he frowned.

"I'm more real than you are. You're just rumours and hearsay, a hallucination."

"Does that matter?"

"If I rub my eyes, you'll disappear. You were never here in the first place." He closed his eyes and pinched the thin skin on the inside of his elbow, but he felt the pain and didn't wake up.

When he opened his eyes, the Angels were still there.

"Eric Solomon," they boomed, in a voice that demanded attention.

He looked at them imperiously. "You're real," he whispered.

"We know that you are a sinner. You have wasted your life by drinking away the nights, bloated with lust for actresses and models. You have worshipped false idols, from musicians to cartoon characters. You have lied, cheated, stolen, and swindled your way through life."

Solomon raised his hand to interrupt them, but they continued to talk as if he weren't even there. The Angels didn't raise their voices – they just refused to be unheard. It was as though they were talking silently and he was listening with his soul.

"You have committed each of the seven sins and an endless number of others. Your apocalypse is now. Do you have anything to say in your defence? Will you repent? Will you kneel and beg for forgiveness before the sheepdogs of the Lord? Justify yourself."

"Why should I?" he cried.

"If you do not, you will be purged."

"What happened to a fair trial?"

"We are a fair trial. Speak." It wasn't a command, but Solomon felt compelled to answer.

"'I've enjoyed myself, isn't that the point? I've led a happy life and been nice enough to the people I've known. I've never been violent and I've always worked hard, I'm just down on my luck at the moment. There's a recession."

"We know everything and more."

"Then you already know what's going to happen?"

"Correct. But knowledge of the future is not meant for you. Do you have anything else to add to your defence?"

"I'm not afraid to die." Solomon sighed and stood tall, a fraction of his former self.

Without seeming to move, the Angels grew nearer, and Solomon was surrounded. He could feel the heat from their bodies and see the wall-mounted clock through their translucent flesh. He stared at the second hand; it ticked, and the Angels stepped through him.

Solomon shrieked as white-hot pain passed through him, and he whimpered as he smelled his own burning flesh. He thought that the pain was unbearable; then, it intensified. The Angels were strengthened by his imminent death, and their bodies started to solidify. Solomon slipped into an unconsciousness from which he'd never wake, and the Angels caught his falling body with ease.

As they held him, draped across their arms like a battered rug, he ignited. None of the Angels flinched; they stood, staring at the fire, with an inscrutable expression on their androgynous faces. In the distance, a car horn honked impatiently. Seconds later, it sounded again; the flames began to die down, Solomon's body reduced to dust and ash.

"You lied, Mr. Solomon," they said, scattering the powdered remains across the floor. "You *were* afraid to die."

The Angels walked towards the wall, passing through it as the widescreen television behind them continued to broadcast static, and the eerie sound kept the ashes company.

# CHAPTER TWO: ROBERT JONES' EDITORIAL, *THE TELEGRAPH*

*Friday January 1st, 2010*

NO-ONE KNOWS when the attacks started, but they grew more frequent towards the end of the year. Likewise, we didn't know what caused them. There were rumours of co-ordinated kidnappings and terrorist plots, but they had no more substance than the whispers that spread them. Conspiracy theorists claimed the attacks were the work of an Orwellian secret society, hell-bent on changing the world by removing one person at a time. The truth was, we were all stumped.

There are no statistics because the Angels never officially existed. The whole world was riding the Mary Celeste, and no-one knew how to drop anchor and signal for help. The police did nothing (how could they fight an unknown enemy?), and the politicians claimed that the problems were caused by the public. But they couldn't explain the reports from African tribesmen or quarantined scientists at faraway research stations. How could these people perpetuate the hoax if they hadn't heard of it?

It happened everywhere. The rumours spread across the globe and were met with universal derision. *El Fantasma, Les Séraphins, Der Schleichender Tod* – The Angels. We didn't know what to think, so we tried not to think at all. By the beginning of December, the number of global disappearances surpassed 100,000, but authorities refused to act.

More people attended churches, prayer meetings, and ceremonies, driven to religion by fear of the unknown. Occasionally, the papers wrote about isolated communities disappearing overnight, and alcoholism and drug addiction were at an all-time high. Society was falling apart, and no-one knew how to stop it.

# CHAPTER THREE: AN OLD FRIEND

*Wednesday November 18th, 2009*

**ROBERT JONES PARKED** his brand new Beamer in the empty churchyard and sighed. The petrol light was flashing, but that wasn't why he stopped. His head ached from prescription drugs and complicated spreadsheets, and his body was vibrating again. The palpitations were getting worse, but he wouldn't have it looked at. Robert's school of thought was old-fashioned – as long as he was breathing, why worry?

Jones twisted the key and cut the ignition, feeling his headache subside with the radio. He reached for his cigarettes and stepped out of the car, pausing to collect his cold Starbucks from the cup-holder. He flicked a button on the keys and walked away, not bothering to wait for the chirp of the central locking. Potential theft didn't bother him – he knew this part of London like the back of his hand, and he loved it like a father.

Robert felt unholy as he walked across the grounds with a cigarette in hand, wondering whether priests hid nicotine-stained fingernails inside their pockets. Almost unconsciously, he drained his coffee and threw the cup into a litter bin.

Walking through the tiny graveyard that skirted the southern wall of the rectory, Jones paused to read the inscriptions, daydreaming about the people that inspired them. He remembered stashing whiskey behind one of the stones as a teenager and cursed himself with a mixture of disgust and regret.

Jones finished his cigarette with a long drag and flicked it over the mossy wall before pushing open the heavy doors and slipping inside. It was his private place – apart from the tired-eyed vicar; it was rare to see another face, and he'd known Father Montgomery forever.

He sat on a pew by the door and closed his eyes, more from exhaustion than in prayer. A couple of rows in front, a timid old lady uttered a quiet salutation to a statue of the Virgin Mary. She didn't look well, and Jones wondered whether she'd always been religious. She looked the type, with her pious optimism in the face of the blatant, depressing truth. She was dying, he knew.

Those troubled thoughts were interrupted by heavy footsteps, and Jones turned to see the wizened figure of Father Montgomery weaving through the pews towards him. He always looked out of place in his robes – his nose had been broken in a schoolyard fight, and he dyed his greying hair. Fit for a man in his sixties, he believed in a strict regime of mental and physical fitness.

"Robert!" Father Montgomery exclaimed, shaking his visitor's hand. "How are you? I haven't seen you for months. What have you been doing with yourself?"

"Oh, you know – the usual. Peterson's backing an important bid, so I've been stuck in meeting after meeting. No-one wants to take the risk because of the recession."

"Sounds like a nightmare," the priest replied.

"It's no worse than usual. I sometimes dream about quitting."

"You shouldn't. You've worked too hard to throw it all away."

"Yeah, you're probably right," Jones said. He noticed that the old woman had finished her prayers, and he remembered how fragile she looked. Nodding at her, he asked Father Montgomery, "Is she okay?"

"Mrs. Forbes? She's having a tough time. Her husband died in January, and she's just been diagnosed with cancer. They gave her three months to live."

"Jesus Christ," whispered Jones, and he immediately regretted it. He'd been raised to be respectful.

"She comes here when she's lonely, but there's only me to talk to. Even that'll stop, soon. Strictly speaking, she should be in a hospice."

"There's no justice," Jones muttered, shaking his head. "How are things with you?"

"I've been bored. I know I shouldn't say it, but nothing happens here. People just aren't religious, these days."

The old priest spent his time working on sermons that no-one ever listened to.

Jones shifted uncomfortably, a disbeliever. "You should get the locals involved. Back in the day, the church was the pillar of the community, right? I bet this place would be full of people if they knew it was here."

The old man smiled, wanly. "We both know that's not true. People don't care anymore. My friend, I'm a fossil."

"I'll visit more often."

"No," replied the priest. "You've got your career to worry about, and a child to support. I don't need charity. I'm supposed to give, not receive. How is your boy, anyway?"

"Kate doesn't let me see him, but he's probably better off without me. Maybe if I just keep paying the child support—"

"You should meet with her," Montgomery interrupted. "Talk it through. You can't keep living like this."

"I know. But I can't look after him at the moment. He's better off without me."

Montgomery touched Jones' arm and glanced at his face with concern in his wise eyes. "What do you mean? Are you all right?"

"I'm fine," Jones replied, feeling faint. "I can look after myself."

"You can talk to me at any time. I'll always be here if you need me."

"Of course, Father. Thank you."

Jones felt the priest's sad eyes on his back, following him as he walked away. Back in the car, he lit a cigarette before gunning the engine and driving towards a meeting that he hadn't prepared for.

# CHAPTER FOUR: THE LARGE HADRON COLLIDER

*Wednesday September 10th, 2008*

**DEEP UNDERGROUND,** surrounded by thick windows and expensive machinery, Professor Klaus Boerman was sitting impatiently in an uncomfortable chair, waiting for his assistant to return. Excitement coursed through him like an electric current in a puddle, and he shook with built-up adrenaline. *This is the most important thing I'll ever do*, he thought, bracing himself for the responsibility.

The computer screen read 10:22. *Where the hell is she? Six minutes to go.* Fleur didn't really need to be there, but this would only happen once. She'd never forgive herself if she missed it.

Boerman looked around and saw the same pent-up excitement in the faces of the crowd that surrounded him. Half of them had spent their academic life in pursuit of this moment, and the other half were simply lucky. A hand on his shoulder made him jump, and he looked round to see the tall, slim figure of Fleur Montmaison, clutching a cup of coffee and grinning behind her horn-rimmed spectacles.

"I thought you'd like a drink," she explained, her accent thicker than the sludge that came out of the dispensers. "Did I miss anything?"

Boerman accepted the Styrofoam cup with thanks and burned his tongue as he took a sip. "No, you're here just in time."

As though he'd heard overheard the conversation, the chief co-ordinator cupped his hands around his mouth. Vince was a fearsome man – six feet tall with Celtic red hair and a flowing crimson beard.

"Five minutes to go," he bellowed. "To your positions. Get ready to witness history."

There was a flurry of activity, and Boerman handed the coffee back to his young assistant.

"No rest for the wicked," he said, sliding back onto his seat before the screen.

Behind him, he could hear the humming of a hundred other physicists, all eager to witness the scientific event of the new millennium. He felt Fleur's presence behind him, and it reassured him. As a rule, he didn't work with a team, but he'd been with her ever since he'd got the job.

"Three minutes to go, take your places."

People were still slipping into the room, but they were unimportant. Everyone that mattered was in place. The late arrivals were a mixture of support staff, assistants, and journalists. They were just there to see the show, not to take part in it.

"Hey Vince," shouted Alvarez, a chubby little man in a sharp suit. "You look worried. Anyone would think this is important!"

A couple of people laughed, but the co-ordinator smiled humourlessly and said nothing.

*Well*, Boerman reflected. *I'm in place. Not that it'll do much good.* Most of the work was done by the computers, and he'd only need to concentrate if something went wrong and the engineers had to override the system. With the meticulous planning that led to the Collider's construction, that seemed unlikely. Boerman's real job was to oversee the technical readouts and to look impressive for the press. The eyes of the world were upon them, and everyone was holding their breath.

"One minute!" shouted the co-ordinator, and an electronic countdown began.

The journalists looked excited, but the CERN staff had practiced this moment and maintained their professional veneer.

"Thirty seconds!"

"Until the world explodes," joked Alvarez, and everybody laughed.

The scientists were at ease, but some members of the press exchanged nervous glances. Their TV stations and newspapers had helped to fuel the unfounded rumours of miniature black holes that could destroy the world. At fifteen seconds, the sweat started to pour from Boerman's brow. *Here we go*, he thought. It reached zero, and a furious cheer erupted as the computer screens began to fill with data.

"Congratulations, gentlemen," shouted the co-ordinator, allowing the din to die down. "We're on!"

Another cheer, almost as loud as the first, filled the enormous room, accompanied by the manic flashes of a score of eager photographers. Boerman tapped half-heartedly at the computer terminal – the readouts were to his satisfaction.

"That was exciting." He turned to look at Fleur, who was calm and composed as usual.

She offered him the rapidly-cooling coffee and he took it back with steady hands, leaning away from the terminal in case he spilled it and became front-page news across the world. There were countless fail-safes in place, but he didn't want to give the press an unnecessary story, especially if it would cast CERN in a bad light.

"Yeah, it was," he replied, draining the coffee and handing the Styrofoam cup back to her. "Do you realise, this is the most important thing that will ever happen to us? In a passive way, we're part of history. We're like the slaves that built the pyramids. We took part. That's the crucial thing, do you see? It would have happened without us, but we put the final stone at the top."

"Nice analogy," she said.

"Now the real work begins," he continued, ignoring her. "It's time to begin the gentler and more refined process of decorating and fitting our temple to the Higgs boson. First, we have to find it."

"Do you think we will?"

"I'm not sure. Nobody knows, how could they? What about you, do you think we'll find it?"

She looked around lazily, as though searching for the answer on one of the terminals.

"Or..." she said, gazing into space. "Do you think it'll find us?"

# CHAPTER FIVE: A DAY AT THE ZOO

*Wednesday September 2nd, 2009*

**"ANGELICA?** Get over here right now!"

"Okay!" The energetic eight-year-old ran to her mother and left the tigers to their afternoon nap. "Can I have an ice cream?"

"We'll see. Your father wants to take a photograph. Put that down, you don't know where it's been."

Angelica opened her mouth to argue, but she saw the look in her mother's eyes and decided against it. A mahogany charm dropped from her fingers and landed in the mud. Carved into the wood, a hideous Angel stared into the dirt.

A camera flashed, but it was a warm day and the sunlight swallowed it. No-one bothered to look at the photograph – they'd already taken hundreds. Angelica's mother took her daughter by the hand and dragged her away again.

"Darling, do you want to see the meerkats?"

"I want to see the monkeys," she replied, so they walked through the reptile house towards the other end of the zoo.

They walked past animals they'd never heard of, past the elephant enclosure where an Indian giant slept in the sunshine, and through a narrow walkway to the primates.

"Look at them, they're huge!"

"I've never liked gorillas," said her father, stroking his stubble and adjusting his spectacles. "Strange creatures. Their arms are like tennis balls in tights."

Angelica inched closer to the cage – if she stretched, she could just reach the metal mesh. It felt surprisingly cool under the late summer sun. Inside the enclosure, the alpha male crawled across on his powerful haunches until his sad face was barely a metre away from Angelica's. A spark of recognition passed between them, and their eyes glued together. Angelica's head burned, and she clutched at her ears with delicate hands, her hazel eyes snapping shut as the gorilla's irises flashed red. She was ready to scream, but the pain disappeared when her father lifted her up and propped her on his shoulder.

"Come on then, trouble. What else shall we have a look at?"

"I want to see the pandas!"

"Then what are we waiting for? Let's go!"

As the family walked away, they didn't look back. The gorilla cowered behind his powerful hands and whimpered like a dog in a thunderstorm.

Two days later, it was dead.

# CHAPTER SIX: FATHER MONTGOMERY'S LECTURE

*Tuesday September 8th, 2008*

**TODAY, WE'RE TALKING ABOUT** the Higgs boson particle, the 'God' particle that the CERN scientists are trying to isolate. People say that the machine will lead to the destruction of mankind. Many Catholics have attacked scientists for their 'blasphemy,' and professors are acting like intellectual police and dismissing good people, determined to slow the inevitable march of scientific progress. The question on the minds of many is...

...who is telling us the truth?

The answer, my friends, is simple. In our society, white lies are commonplace and black ones are rarely confronted. Ignorance isn't bliss, but people accept it because it's easier than facing up to reality. It's time for us to demand the truth.

First and foremost, we need to know more about the particle. How can something so small be so controversial? Critics say that scientists coined the nickname, but that's untrue. Why would they break their countless rules and naming conventions for the Higgs boson? As with most of the evil in the world, the name was fabricated by the media.

So, what is the Higgs boson particle? Even its existence is still under debate, so it's little more than a theory. It's believed to be an integral part of the world that we see before us, and if it really does exist, it would help to explain the origins of mass in our universe. Mass, as we all know, is something that Catholics feel strongly about. But that's the communion wine and the body of the Lord, not the scientific concept that links with gravity to give an object weight. Scientists say that the Higgs boson particle is expected to explain the moment of creation.

Many Christians argue that the Higgs boson will (if discovered) disprove the existence of God, but that simply isn't true. If anything, it'll show us the techniques that he used, and that shouldn't be blasphemous or heretical. Does it matter whether we understand creation, as long as we don't claim its beauty for ourselves? Are there some things that man should never know?

Friends, CERN's research is no more un-Christian than Newton's forays into gravitational pull or the orbits of the planets. Science and religion are code-words for an ancient search for understanding, and they ought to go hand-in-hand. Should we condemn scientists for trying to better their understanding of the universe that God created? You tell me. I, for one, find it difficult to lay blame at their feet.

To the thousands of people involved in the project, it could be an academic pursuit or the realisation of a life-long dream. For others, it's a way to bring science and religion together, whether as friends or as enemies. In the end, we have to look within ourselves to find our feelings on the matter. If we are strong and faithful, we can support this research until the end, whatever the outcome.

# CHAPTER SEVEN: RETRIBUTION

*Tuesday November 24th, 2009*

**VINCENT FOSTER,** senior co-ordinator at CERN, looked around nervously as he walked out of the building and over to his car. Only last month, he would've paused to admire the leather seats and shiny alloys, but he had no time for that now. Something strange was happening, and he didn't like it.

The scientist thought he was being followed. A man who believed in logic, he wasn't paranoid, but he saw shadows during the night. They weren't professionals, he could tell. Even when they stood in darkness, his stalkers seemed to stand out. He shivered.

He'd noticed them a month ago, not long after the first collisions in the LHC. Then, he'd dismissed them as the products of an over-worked imagination, but they kept coming back. He'd even been to the police, but they didn't take him seriously. They sent an officer to search the area and found nothing unusual – no footprints and no suspects to support his story.

Then, he'd been followed to work, and he started to see them at the side of the road, watching as he drove past. The dark feeling of constant surveillance had been building up for weeks, and it was slowly beginning to gnaw at his concentration. His colleagues had noticed a difference, and his performance was suffering. After a tense meeting, he'd been given three weeks of paid leave and had been asked to come back refreshed or not at all. He planned to take the opportunity to barricade himself inside the basement of his rented apartment.

As he climbed into his car on that chilly November night, he was finalising his plans. He'd anticipated this moment for weeks, stocking up on bottled water and tinned food. Foster strapped himself in and gunned the engine, then glanced around again, squinting through the darkness. Was there someone in the shadows, softly illuminated by an invisible light? By the time that he swept the trees with his headlights, the figure had disappeared.

"Come on then," he muttered, locking his doors. "Where are you?" After scouring the area, he decided that they weren't coming back. Shaking his head, he pulled out of the car park and started the long drive back to his fortress.

The roads wound through small villages that were built into the mountainside, and the scientist had never grown tired of the journey. Now, things were different. He barely noticed his surroundings as he sped along the road in the darkness, formulating new schemes for survival. *I'm losing my mind*, he thought, stroking his bearded chin.

His car rolled through a sleeping village, and he wished that the streetlights were on. His headlights illuminated the road before him, but he couldn't see much else. Occasionally, he thought he saw a face amongst the trees, but that could've been a trick of the moonlight. He felt like a gazelle trying to outrun a pack of lions.

Anxiety suddenly pushed him to drive faster, whipping around the narrow corners at a hundred kilometres an hour. He knew he could drive, but it was a long time since he'd been a reckless teenager, pushing his car to the limits under the glare of the baking Australian sun. Now, he was relying on that long-forgotten talent to take him away from his unknown adversaries.

As he swerved around a corner and struggled with the vehicle, he saw them. Most of them were peering around the thick trunks of the gigantic trees that were anchored to the slopes of the mountainside, but two of them stood shoulder-to-shoulder forty metres in front of him, frozen and unresponsive in the road. He couldn't avoid them – it was too late for that. Foster slammed his foot on to the brake, but he already knew it was useless.

The Citroen flew forward, and Foster pressed back against his seat, preparing himself for an impact that never came. Even through his terror, he was too morbidly fascinated to close his eyes. When the car was centimetres away, the Angels disappeared, vanishing as if they'd never been there at all. Foster blinked; his foot was still jammed against the brake, and he slowed softly to a halt in the middle of the narrow road.

For a few brief moments, he saw nothing but the night. Then, like something from a nightmare, two figures materialised in the darkness and began to walk towards the stricken automobile. They shone, as always, and Foster was too terrified to move. An ethereal, harmonious voice whispered to him, wiser than a library and older than a thousand fossils.

"Wait," it seemed to say. "Wait for us to reach you."

With a mighty effort, he took his eyes off the mirror and eased the car forwards. He started slowly, but when he saw more of them climbing from behind the trees, he accelerated around the corner and raced home. As he turned, he could still see them on the road, striding purposefully towards him. He didn't apply the brakes until he pulled onto the drive.

\*   \*   \*

The crunch of pebbles beneath the tyres sounded like the breaking of bones. The noise used to relax him, but now he felt desolate and alone. The darkness swallowed him whole as he fumbled with his keys on the doorstep. As Foster marched determinedly around the corner, several of the spectres stared in his direction. He patted his pockets, searching for his mobile phone.

"Damn," he cursed. "It's in the car."

Somehow, he unlocked the door and bolted it behind him, before hitting the light switch with a trembling hand. His gaze darted around the hallway; only his reflection looked back at him. In the kitchen, he picked up a carving knife and ran across the floorboards towards the stiff cellar door. He kicked it open, locked it behind him with a rusty key, and ran down the stone steps. Foster tried to forget that he was outnumbered, that he was scared and alone and afraid to take a life, if that's what it came to.

He sat with his back against the cold, stone wall, staring at the stairwell and the doorway. This was where he'd make his stand, surrounded by tinned food and crates of water. In one corner, a camp-bed was already made, and the whole place was rancid with dampness and fear.

After fifteen minutes, he was still waiting in the half-light, and his heart-rate was gradually slowing. He heard nothing from above and wondered if they'd given up pursuit. Foster tilted his head to one side and heard nothing but a distant melody on the wind. Silently, the assault began.

Two pairs of spectral feet sank through the concrete roof, and Vincent Foster squealed with terror and surprise. The rest of the bodies soon followed, like unholy stalactites reaching for the floor. The co-ordinator was too scared to move, so he stared at the fiends in front of him.

"Wait." To ignore the command was unthinkable. "The others are coming, and you will wait."

The words buzzed around his skull and he knew that they were true. The others would come, and nothing he could do would change it.

Seconds later, more Angels drifted through the ceiling. He couldn't look at them directly – he had to stare at them from the corner of his eye. *What the hell is happening?* He looked at the situation like a scientist. *I suppose reality is subjective.*

"Reality is subjective," they said, in a shared voice that reverberated eerily around the room.

*Impossible,* he thought. *They can't know what I'm thinking.*

"Mr. Foster, nothing is impossible. Merely improbable."

"Who are you?" he asked, his voice clear and calm, though his heart was raging against his ribcage.

"We have no name, just a purpose."

"And what's your purpose?"

"We exist to purge the universe of unworthy life-forms. In terms that you will understand, we are the auditors of intelligent thought. You must justify yourself. Why should we let you live?"

"You murder?"

"A human crime. We do not murder, we judge."

As one, the Angels pressed forwards. Foster thrust at them with the blade of his knife, which passed easily through flesh. It happened in slow motion. The stricken Angel didn't flinch, but Foster's arm began to sizzle and he drew back in blinding agony.

The Angel smiled with a sad wisdom. His flesh grew cloudier until Foster could see through him to the wall on the other side. The scientist blanched with incredulity – the knife was lodged in the translucent void where the Angel's stomach should have been. Smoke poured from it like dry ice on a movie set, and the blade burst into bright flames. It burned quickly and ferociously until the molten steel fell to the floor and began to eat its way through the concrete.

"What's happening?" he asked, but his disjointed mind didn't want an answer.

"Do you understand now?" they asked.

Foster shook his head.

"Very well. You may ask us three questions, and then you must tell us why you deserve to live."

"Three questions?"

"That is correct. What is your second question?"

Foster realised his mistake and cried aloud, but it was already too late to change it. He surrendered the question without argument and focused his intellect on the two that still remained.

"What are you?"

"We have no name, but your countrymen will grow to call us 'Angels'. We are not defined by our names, but you may define us by our purpose. We exist to free the universe from sin."

"I see," said the scientist, though he didn't. "Sounds too biblical for me."

The Angels merely glared at him with inscrutable faces.

"And your third question?"

"That one's easy. Where did you come from?"

"You released us," they answered, and he gasped. "You woke us from our eternal slumber. Your day of judgement is coming, and we are holding the gavel."

"I don't understand," he said, the shadow of his former self. "How did I release you? What did I release you from?"

"No more questions – justify your existence."

"And what if I can't?"

"Justify your existence."

"How did I 'release' you?" he pleaded.

"Justify your existence."

"Not until—" he began, but he was cut short.

Their leader reached out in a Nazi salute and clenched his fist so tightly that it could've melted matter. Foster dropped to the floor, dead. His heart had combusted inside his chest, charred beyond recognition, an un-solvable riddle for an autopsy team.

The Angels left the way they had come, nonchalant and determined, floating through the roof like the final breaths of a dying man. They didn't look back.

# CHAPTER EIGHT: A CLANDESTINE MEETING

*Thursday November 15th, 1962*

**MONTGOMERY DRAGGED** a comb through his dark, unruly hair and examined himself in the mirror. He didn't look handsome, just pious and respectable. His hair, after preening, looked presentable, and his twenty-year-old face was set in an expression of sorrow. He pressed his trousers and ironed his shirt, shined his shoes until his fingers hurt, then sighed.

He glanced at the clock, though he already knew the time – he had to leave. Casting a tired eye around the room, he spied a bottle of gin beside his prayer book, mocking the communion wine. It was emptier than he would've liked, but he picked it up and drained it anyway, wincing as the liquid fire ravaged his throat. He cried sweat, but he needed courage.

At the washbasin, he squeezed a pea of toothpaste onto a finger and rubbed it across his teeth. *I wasn't expecting this*, he thought. He lived at a seminary in a sleepy Scottish town, slowly adjusting to his minimalist lifestyle. When he wasn't studying, he was working, volunteering in the community to serve his people. It was demanding work, and it left him drained and lethargic. The bags under his eyes were from sleepless nights and busy days.

With a sigh, he picked up his leather shoulder-bag and walked out of the door. He didn't bother to lock it – no-one steals from a priest. Before long, he was walking out of the compound.

He was a mile away and running late, but he didn't hurry – he wasn't looking forward to the meeting. His thoughts wandered with him, and he asked himself, "Am I doing the right thing?"

Sarah was already there when he arrived, a hunched figure on a bench with her back to the sun. Her mousy hair was tied in a bland ponytail, and her overcoat looked like a prop from a detective movie. She wore a hat, and her slender hands were hidden beneath delicate gloves.

"Hello," she said, rising unsteadily to greet him.

Montgomery reached for her arm, but she pushed him away irately.

"No, don't touch me."

He looked at her and smiled, sadly.

"Of course," he said. "I'm sorry."

Sarah tried to climb from her seat, but her body was still too frail.

"How are you holding up?" Montgomery asked.

"I've been better," she replied. "No matter what happens, I can't go back."

"I know. Where have you been?"

"With my parents. Father thinks I'm a disappointment, I can see it in his eyes."

Montgomery's brow furrowed as she spoke – he'd never liked the old man, but this was a new low.

"Mother says nothing, but I know she doesn't want me. The convent won't take me back, and none of my friends will speak to me."

"I'm sorry."

"It was my fault, too. I just feel so tired."

Montgomery said nothing, thinking desperately.

"And now we must decide what to do. I presume that's why you're here."

"I wanted to make sure that you were all right," he said.

"I'm not all right."

"I know." The conversation faded to an awkward silence. Montgomery bit his fingernails until he could contain himself no longer. "So what are we going to do?"

"What do you mean?"

"With our son," he replied. "What are you proposing?"

"Quiet!" she barked, looking around nervously.

Straight away, he knew what was going to happen. Sarah had nothing left to lose, but he could lose it all. Their doomed affair was compromised, but she didn't have to drag him down with her. Montgomery felt almost tranquil.

Sarah was still incensed. "Couldn't you find somewhere more private?"

"I come here when I want to be alone."

"But what if we're caught? If the truth comes out then there's no turning back."

"Where else could we go? No, we stay here." He bit his lip and cast a glum eye over the skyline.

Then they looked at each other, and a spark of intensity passed between them. Sarah tried to smile, but it looked more like a grimace. She took a deep breath before continuing.

"There's nothing else we can do. I told them that I didn't know the father's name. I hope you realise what that means. But I had to do it, to protect you."

Montgomery paused and allowed the enormity of her sacrifice to sink in. She was subjecting herself to the scorn and rejection of her friends and family so that his own name would remain clean. He wanted to apologise, but he couldn't.

Instead, he fixed his eyes on hers and whispered, "Are you sure that you know what you're doing?"

"No, I'm just trying to do some good. The church has treated me badly, but I still believe in love. I'm going to give the baby up for adoption."

A tear trickled from the corner of her eye, but her sad voice stayed steady.

Montgomery didn't know what to say – he didn't even know how to feel. "Is there no other way?"

"Not that I can see. Just think about it. It's the best option. You can continue your training, and I can move away."

"What about our son?"

Her face flushed. "I'll put him in an orphanage. It's the best thing for him. I don't want him to be the bastard son of the village whore. Neither do you."

"You're not a whore," he whispered.

"You and I know that, but what about the rest of the world? Think about it, then tell me I'm being heartless. I love my son," she said, crying openly. "But I want him to be happy and successful. I can't even support myself. He'll be better off without me."

Montgomery didn't know what to say, so he took a seat beside her and covered his face with his hands. Neither spoke for several minutes – instead, they listened to the singing of the birds and the distant hum of the traffic.

Finally, Montgomery spoke. "I'll come with you."

# CHAPTER NINE: A NEW DEVELOPMENT

*Thursday September 10th, 2009*

**IN THE DARK ROOM** in the back of Jessops, the sales manager took his tongue out of the new intern's mouth for long enough to speak.

"You'll never believe this," he said. "I've never seen anything like it."

"What is it?"

The manager grabbed a wad of negatives and waved them under the intern's prominent nose. "A bunch of photographs?"

"Just take a look at them."

The photographs showed a young family on a day out, laughing and joking with endless ice creams. The mother was beautiful, with deep hazel eyes and long, blonde hair; the father was stern and chiselled, with a face that spoke of long nights of hard work and years of dedication. But their daughter – she was something else.

"It's the same in every picture," he explained, leafing through the stack. "The way her face blurs and distorts, it's terrifying."

"Don't talk like that," she said. "You're scaring me."

"It gets weirder – look at the background, do you see what I see?"

"It's blurry..." She leaned in closer and adjusted the crooked spectacles on her nose.

"Yeah," he replied. "But they're definitely people – at least, they're shaped like people. They're following them, look."

It was true. In every photograph, the figures lurked in the background and watched over the family like prison wardens.

She looked at the manager in alarm. "Should we tell someone?"

"Like who? Who should we tell? No, it's pointless. Even with the photos, people would find an explanation. It's probably just a trick of the light." He slipped them back into the envelope and chucked it across the room. "We're not paid to think. Let's just get back to business."

As he eased himself back in to her, they were too deep in the thrall of a mutual climax to notice their surroundings, but the Angels were in no hurry. They watched in grim silence from the walls until the fleeting sin was completed. Then they burned the photographs and prepared to pass judgement.

# CHAPTER TEN: A CLIPPING FROM THE OBSERVER

*Friday November 20th, 2009*

## UNEXPLAINED DISAPPEARANCES ON THE RISE

UNOFFICIAL REPORTS of mysterious disappearances are sweeping the nation, as the public pressures the government to investigate.

Third-party estimates suggest a substantial increase in the number of missing persons, and anonymous sources from the Metropolitan Police Force have supported the claims.

The whistle-blowers are not the only ones to worry. In a recent press release, Scotland Yard stated, "We ask the public not to report a crime unless [they're] sure that a crime has actually been committed."

Meanwhile, local councils are understaffed and over-budget.

"Most of our regular patrols have been called off," confessed an anonymous MP. "And nobody will tell us what's happening."

According to some, there's a sinister force at work.

"It's the Angels," said mastodon444, a self-proclaimed member of 'hacktivist' group *Anonymous*. "They're coming for us all. We don't understand the true meaning of the Bible. Angels aren't 'angelic,' after all."

He goes on to explain the theory – that a secret, international group of terrorists is carrying out co-ordinated kidnappings. Their motivation is unclear, but ours isn't the only country to be affected. In France, they have *Les Séraphins Maléfiques*; in Germany, *Der Schleichender Tod*. The attacks are spreading across Africa, Asia, Europe, Australia, and the Americas. Many supporters of the theory believe that this should be enough to force the British government to investigate.

Whatever the truth, it's clear that the pressure is on for the authorities to provide an explanation. So far, Downing Street is silent.

# CHAPTER ELEVEN: BEINGS OF LIGHT

*Sunday November 15th, 2009*

**MONTGOMERY STAYED BEHIND** long after the service, sweeping the floors and adjusting the religious displays. In the glory days, they'd had a cleaner; now, the church was falling apart. It was tiring, but the priest worked hard to look after the place himself. He liked the hallowed silence that the church offered, and he wished he were strong enough to carry out repairs. As it was, he satisfied himself by dragging an old broom across the dusty stone and polishing every surface he could reach.

It started on a quiet November night. Most people had to work in the morning, and those who didn't were kept inside by the cold air and the dark sky. Cars rumbled hypnotically past, as easy to ignore as a ticking clock.

He was wiping down shelves in the old rectory when he heard the commotion. For centuries, the room had mostly been used for storage, but meetings were occasionally held there. Strange noises startled him, but the courage and curiosity of his youth prevailed. His old brain decoded the pattering of running feet, and a pair of heavy fists smashed against the door.

"Father!"

The voice had a thick Irish accent, and it radiated panic and despair. The oak portal rattled in its hinges, and Montgomery raced towards it, wrenching the rusty bolts back and fumbling with the key. When the bolts snapped open, the door flew out and almost knocked the Irishman over. As soon as the drunk was over the threshold, Montgomery slammed the door behind him and jammed the bolts home.

"Ah," said Montgomery, calm and composed in the face of insanity. "Niall. And what can I do for you?"

"They're after me, Father," Niall whimpered, grabbing Montgomery's arm and steering him into the shadows. "I seen 'em, I really did."

"Calm down. What is it?" The lairy Irishman was a notorious drunk, and Montgomery often looked after him. Niall didn't have a home, so he slept on the floor in the rectory. This arrangement was under threat since he'd been caught with the communion wine.

"I seen 'em, Father. All in a line behind the bushes. Well, we've all heard about 'em, sure enough. It's all anybody talks about, these days."

"Slow down, Niall. Start from the beginning."

"Sure thing, Father," he said. "They can't set foot in the house of the Lord. We've got all the time in the world."

The priest was used to the Irishman's ramblings, but he normally flowed through topics as though the boundaries didn't exist. For once, Niall made sense – sort of.

"You were being followed?"

"You don't know the half of it. It's these Angels. That's what I reckon."

"I've heard of them," Montgomery said, and he had. Half of the country was alive with the rumour. "Go on, I'm listening."

"There I was, sitting in the car park and minding my own business. You know how it is, Father. I was drinking my medicine, if you catch my drift."

"I understand."

"Out of nowhere, this fella comes up to me... I thought he was the fuzz until I found my glasses and got a proper look. D'you know what, Father? He was naked, I'll swear it. Naked as the day he was born. He was handsome, though. Reminded me of my younger days." Now that the sense of imminent danger had passed, Niall was settling into the story.

Montgomery was patient though, and he said nothing as he parsed reality from the tale.

"He was a strange fella, and not just 'cause he was naked. He seemed to shine. I thought I was seeing things. It's happened before, it's the nature of the beast. It was like he was lit up by a spotlight, only more like he was the spotlight, and I was on the stage."

"Did he say what he wanted?"

"You see, that's the weird thing... he did. He had a deep voice that echoed like he was standing inside the church. And he said to me, 'Justify yourself.' Then he told me to wait, and I was just about to run. He said there were more on their way, and that's all I needed to know. I'm telling you, it was hard to move my legs."

"Catatonia," Montgomery murmured. "Interesting."

"And then he said, if you'll believe me, 'His fear is building. Follow him, but don't catch him yet. This fruit is not yet fully ripe.' Well, Father, that got me moving all right. I ran across town and they followed me all the way here. They ain't coming inside the church, though. They wouldn't dare."

But Montgomery was no longer listening. He could hear voices through the walls, and he sidled over to the door to listen. He wondered if *they* were real. Could the drunkard's tale be a trick? Cautiously, he slid the bolts across and opened the door, peering out into the darkness. He couldn't see anything unusual.

"Hello?" he called, but there was no response except for the faint echo, which mimicked his gentle accent and faded into the night. He tried again, and then a third time, but nothing changed. It was raining, and a fine mist was rising from the river and tickling the horizon. He called one last time, before giving up and returning to the warmth.

The old Irishman had slumped to the floor and fallen into a dazed half-sleep in his absence, and Montgomery frowned at the recumbent figure like a mother at an unruly child. It was getting late, and it wouldn't be easy to take Niall to the shelter. With the long, deep sigh of an impatient man, he grabbed Niall's legs and dragged him to the corner.

The Irishman smelled like a distillery, and the priest marvelled at his aptitude as a drunken raconteur. Montgomery poured a glass of water and stood it beside him, knowing all along that Niall would only touch it if his life depended on it. There was nothing else to do – Montgomery couldn't make the stone floor more comfortable, but comfort was a luxury that Niall could rarely afford. Montgomery's heart was racing, and the rest of the cleaning would have to wait for another day.

He turned off the overhead lights and left Niall on the floor, illuminated by dim side-lights that skirted the great religious precinct and lit the pews. He knew from experience that the church could be unnerving at night, and who knew what hallucinations his alcohol-riddled mind might produce?

Montgomery dismissed the experience as the work of a gullible fool with a drunken imagination, and he felt no fear as he walked through the churchyard in the near-darkness. He left the doors unlocked so Niall could leave, though he'd never left them open before. There wasn't anything worth stealing, but he held a secret dark opinion of human nature. He was a deeply spiritual man, but he was also a realist – faith wouldn't protect the church from graffiti and vandalism.

He was deep in thought as he began the long walk home through the dusty estate. For a fleeting moment, he thought he was being watched, but he shrugged it off and walked calmly through the sleeping city. It was a feeling he was about to get used to.

# CHAPTER TWELVE: THE RENDEZVOUS

*Sunday November 18th, 1962*

**THEY MET AT NIGHT,** on the same bench they had used days earlier. Montgomery's eyes were dark and sunken, and a three-day stubble framed his greasy face with a haunted shadow. He hadn't been sleeping, and his volunteer work was more intense than ever. His team had been carrying out repairs on the youth centre, and his hands were callused and splintered. *You have to suffer for your faith,* he reflected.

He smelled of sweat and cologne, and gin still marred his breath. The lovers communicated in whispers and signals until they were sitting beside each other in the moonlight. No introduction was necessary.

"Are you ready?" asked Montgomery.

Sarah didn't reply – she was biting her fingernails so fiercely that they bled.

Montgomery took a deep breath of fresh air and sighed. "Sarah, are you sure you want to do this?"

In the darkness, the baby started to cry, and Sarah tried her best to comfort it. She loosened the dull straps of the second-hand perambulator and held the child in her arms.

"You know," she began, speaking softly to the night as Montgomery strained to listen. "It's hard to look after a baby that you're giving away."

The child fell silent, and she wrapped it up in a blanket.

"I'll bet," he replied, examining her vague shadow as it rippled across the moonlit grass. "But it's almost over."

"Yes, I suppose it is. It's been a tough week."

Instinctively, Montgomery wrapped his arms around her shoulders, pulling her closer and sheltering her from the persistent wind. She didn't pull away.

"Do you think it would have worked? If things were different?" he asked.

"John, I don't even want to think about it. What's done is done. We're here, and it's now. We don't live in a fairytale." She stood up suddenly and pushed his arm away from her.

"So you don't have feelings for me?"

She was silent for a long time before she answered. "Even if I did, I wouldn't want to talk about it."

"Is it because you're scared of what might happen or because you're scared of what I'll think?" He moved to stand beside her, touching her cheek with a gentle hand.

She shivered, and the moonlight illuminated the goosebumps on her delicate arms. "I just don't know what it would lead to. You don't understand, I have a responsibility to do what's best for our son. Why torment ourselves over what could have been? It didn't happen and that's why we're here."

Montgomery was so close that he could smell the bitter aroma of her flesh, disguised by the perfume that she wore. That was new – when they fell in love, she wasn't allowed to wear it.

"Then let's live in the now and forget about the future. I love you," he whispered.

Sarah tensed up and pulled away from him. The child had stopped crying, and she placed it gently back in the perambulator.

"That's no longer relevant, John. We can't do this, because I'll only drag you down with me." She sighed, and she kissed his cheek with a softness that he didn't know she possessed. "It's just the way things are."

"But couldn't we just..."

"No!" she snapped. "It's over, John. Come on, we have to go."

Montgomery wisely stayed silent.

Pretending not to see her salty tears, he grabbed her arm as she steered the baby through the park. Once they were back out in the open, they pretended not to know each other. Everything was back to normal.

# CHAPTER THIRTEEN: JUST ANOTHER DAY AT THE OFFICE

*Monday November 23rd, 2009*

**JONES WAS BORED,** and boredom was a commodity. He was usually on edge from hard work and caffeine, but he'd been stuck in the office all day, dealing with a backlog of paperwork and watching the cold wind whistle along the pavement. Now it was late, and the office hummed with electricity, revealed by the silence of absent employees.

The telephone rang, and he bent to answer it, but it cut out as his hand touched the receiver. He reached for the handset, dialled 1471 and listened to the automated reply – an internal call from Collins in the managerial suite. He called back, but there was no answer.

He sank back in his seat as a document flashed up on the computer screen. Jones couldn't focus. He'd rather be busy and interested than free to let his mind wander. Collins' office was on the floor above him, it couldn't hurt to visit him in person. Jones scowled at the monitor – now the idea was in his head, he didn't have a choice.

He picked up his lukewarm cup of coffee and walked casually along the corridor, picturing his dinner and reminding himself he was a lucky man. The stairs creaked in the usual place, and Jones paused to take a sip. The building was almost empty, and he enjoyed a brief second of calm solitude on the staircase. Then he saw the lights.

At first, he thought there was a fire, but the yellowish glow looked more like a faulty television set. He moved hypnotically towards it, skulking like a burglar in a swanky suit. He could hear a dozen distant voices, cold and unemotional, and he held his breath as he approached. He wanted to know what was happening. Inching closer, Jones listened in. Something was wrong – he knew it. A crowd was talking, conversing in perfect harmony. It could have been beautiful, but terror took hold of all his senses.

"Tom Collins, we know that you are a liar, a rogue, and a thief. What do you have to say for yourself?"

"I..." Collins sputtered.

Jones heard grotesque desperation and fear of the unknown. The glow filtered through the open door and out into the corridor – it felt unnatural and out of place.

"I don't know what you want me to do," Collins pleaded.

"Justify yourself," the voice replied.

Jones leaned closer.

"I had to do something," Collins begged. "My wife lost her job, my children were hungry. I was a failure. What's the harm in embezzlement? It's the company that loses."

"Theft is a sin. And you cannot lie to us. You have no children, and you have not seen your wife for six years."

Jones shivered and dialled the emergency services from his mobile phone.

"You can't blame me for trying," Collins was saying.

"Hello? Listen closely." Jones was through to the operator, explaining the situation in a whisper and praying that he would be heard as he paused for breath and ordered his thoughts. "I need armed police and an ambulance to 17B Corporation Street, do you hear me?"

Something heavy hit the floor in the next room, and the conversation stopped abruptly. There was a tension in the air that Jones couldn't miss, and he strained his ears and forgot about the telephone. The silence was complete; he couldn't even hear his own rapid heartbeat.

"Hello? Sir?" The operator's tinny voice broke the deafening nothingness, but it was immediately drowned out by a terrible roar of pain and the crackle of burning fat.

The smell filled Jones' nostrils until he remembered nothing else, until vomit leaked from his throat across the hardwood floor. The noise faded into nothingness, and the thunderous rumble of the intruders' voices began.

"You cannot hurt us. You will live to regret your assault on the divine workers. Then, you will die to forget it," the voices threatened.

"Sir? Are you there?" The telephone hung uselessly at Jones' side, and the operator spoke to the palm of his hand.

Jones remembered and brought the mobile to his ear, whispering, "I'm going to have to call you back. Send those cars!"

Another scream echoed along the corridor, and Jones slid his mobile back into his pocket. He wasn't a brave man, but he had a conscience.

Retracing his steps, he ran towards the nearest fire extinguisher and picked it up, wielding it clumsily. He ran back down the corridor and mustered the little courage that he had, before leaping into the room to confront the mysterious assailants.

Robert Jones only needed a second to take in the scene – Collins lying in the corner of the room, still shrieking in pain. Three metres away from him, a computer terminal lay smashed on the floor, the metal case bent and warped. Surrounding the squealing Collins in a semi-circle, pinning him to the corner, a trio of naked men stood with their arms outstretched towards him.

Jones was struck by a sudden realisation – the creatures' flesh was blurred and translucent. They turned their terrifying countenances towards him; a split-second later, a blinding flash shrouded the world in light, and Jones threw his arms across his eyes. When he removed them, he saw little through the haze of ugly spots that the flash had left behind. Collins' tormentors were gone.

"Damn," he cursed, rubbing his eyes like a tired child. "Are you all right, Collins?"

"No," Collins moaned, clutching his badly burned chest with a half-cooked arm. "I think I'm dying."

"You'll be fine." On cue, the distant wail of a police siren leaked through the walls of the building, and Jones looked doubtfully at his colleague. "What happened?"

"Did you see them?" Collins begged as his eyes rolled back into his sockets.

"I did," Jones replied. "Stay with me, buddy. I think you're going into shock. Listen, the police are on their way, and we're going to get you to a hospital. But eventually, someone's going to ask what happened."

Collins groaned and caressed his wounds.

"Tell them the truth."

Jones frowned, then winced as the sirens reached a painful crescendo. It was going to be a long night for both of them, and it wasn't over yet. He stayed by Collins' side until the paramedics arrived.

# CHAPTER FOURTEEN: THE ORPHANAGE

*Sunday November 18th, 1962*

**MR. OATES** drank another glass of whiskey and watched as the children shuffled past in their second-hand clothes. They came from all corners of the capital, sharing nothing but a deep dislike of the system that raised them. Oates was spending his evening in the study with a bottle and the radio, watching juvenile mischief through the open doorway. With a bleak sigh of boredom, he put his head in his hands and tried to think.

When he woke from his drink-fuelled slumber, the hearth held cold ashes and the record player idled beside him. One of the younger boys peered around the doorframe, malevolence etched into his hardened face. Oates climbed unsteadily to his feet, an impressive figure of authority once his posture caught up with his aching brain. The youth ran down the corridor and joined the crowd of milling orphans, and Oates cursed and closed the door. Ten seconds later, he was back in his chair. Twenty seconds later, there was another knock at the door.

"What is it?" he demanded, prowling over to the door and swinging it open in a fury. "Well, what do you want?"

"There's something you need to see."

Oates sobered up immediately. It was Edward Jones, the longest-standing orphan and one of the few boys the old man respected. Secretly, Oates admired Edward's stoicism and unrelenting optimism. At seventeen, Edward was unlikely to find a family.

"What is it?" Oates repeated.

"You'd better take a look, sir. You might not believe me."

"What do you mean?" They took a left and crossed the great hall towards the lawn until the old man suddenly stopped. "I'm not going any further until you tell me what this is all about."

Edward hesitated. "I'll tell you, but we have to keep moving."

"Why?"

"There's a baby, sir. Listen, I'm going to tell the truth. I was out past curfew again. It was on the doorstep when I got home."

Oates sighed, deeply. "Again, boy? And what's this about a baby?"

"We're almost there," Edward said, gesturing to the heavy wooden doors. "If you could do the honours?"

Grudgingly, Oates reached into his deep pockets and pulled out a heavy iron key-ring. Holding it up to the dim bulb, he identified the correct key and unlocked the door with a satisfying click.

The young man led the way to an ivy-covered bench in the courtyard. Oates pushed past and followed his gaze to the moving bundle of rags upon it.

"Well, I'll be damned," he muttered, stooping to pick it up.

The child looked like it was barely a week old. Oates ordered Edward to summon a doctor immediately. He took the child to his study and laid it carefully on the desk. Throughout the ordeal, the baby stayed silent, but it began to cry when Oates bent towards the fire. Cursing, he called down the corridor for help, but nobody came. As a figure of authority, he was despised. The child was still screaming when Edward returned with the doctor, nearly ten minutes later.

"I presume that this is the patient?" The old medic donned his age-worn spectacles and, after a nod from Oates, began to inspect the child. "Another one abandoned, I suppose?"

"Yes," said Edward, before the master had a chance to speak. "I found him outside."

The baby still screamed for the parents who abandoned it, and Oates' head throbbed with the beginnings of a hangover.

"You know what this means?" the doctor asked, reaching into his kit-bag for a stethoscope. "Why don't you tell him, Oates? The old tradition."

"I hardly think it applies," he said, sourly.

"I hardly think it doesn't."

"What tradition?" asked Edward, and the two men turned to look at him. His youthful eyes were on fire with curiosity as he leant eagerly towards them.

Oates gave in with a sigh. "Unwritten rules can always be broken. Traditionally, the duty of naming a foundling falls to the master of this institution, which is me. Tradition," he growled, "dictates that the child takes the surname of the person who found him, which is you."

"Well," interrupted the doctor, finishing his examination and picking up the child with the practiced agility of a professional. "He seems perfectly fine to me, but he's tired. Do you have the facilities to look after him? Your youngest is four, correct?"

"Five. But I suppose we don't have a choice. This is going to create a lot of paperwork and make my life far more difficult, you know?"

"It wasn't me who left him on your doorstep," the doctor said, carrying the baby towards Oates. "Would you mind?"

Oates scowled, but he took the child demurely.

"So, have you decided what to call him?" the doctor asked.

"Jones," said Jones.

Oates glanced carelessly around the room, taking in his bookshelf – two copies of the King James Bible and one of *Treasure Island*. James Jones would never work, so that left only one other choice.

"Robert Jones," he said, with nonchalant finality.

"It's settled." The doctor left the room without a backwards glance, leaving Oates and Edward together. Their eyes met and they shared an uncomfortable moment of silence.

"What do we do now?" Oates asked.

"You mean you don't know?"

\* \* \*

"Did you see that?" The figures were shrouded in darkness, and their eyes glittered in the starlight.

"I did. He's safe."

"Oh, John. Do you think he'll be all right?"

"I can't answer that. But he's in good hands, so let us have faith. The orphanage will be tough, but it should make a man of the boy. Let us pray to that."

They bowed their heads in a silent plea to the god that blessed them with their beautiful curse. All was silent except for the roar of the traffic and the rustling of the bushes.

Sarah sighed and reached for her lover's hand. "Do you ever think we might be wrong?"

"What do you mean?" Montgomery asked.

"There's so much hatred in the world. What's it all for? He has a divine plan, I know. But why isn't it a little… nicer?"

Montgomery had doubts of his own, and he didn't know how to answer. Instead, he pulled her close and tried to protect her from the winter wind.

At last, he spoke. "Everything happens for a reason."

In the darkness, she shivered. "And you believe that? Then you're a bigger fool than I am."

# CHAPTER FIFTEEN: GET WELL SOON

*Friday November 27th, 2009*

**"I JUST DON'T KNOW** what I saw," Jones scowled, as he sat with Montgomery in the rectory, sipping supermarket-brand coffee from chipped mugs. "What do you think I should do? Do you believe me?"

The priest stared intently and nodded his head. "I do. This makes things more interesting."

"It does?"

"I had an unexpected visit from a friend of mine," Montgomery explained, thinking back to the day that Niall sought refuge amongst the pews. "He told a similar story to yours, although I didn't believe him then."

"So why do you believe him now?"

"Because I believe you. Niall is an unfortunate soul, suffering from too many addictions. You'd find it difficult to believe him, too. He looked sincere, but what should you rely on? Hundreds of years of scientific fact or the biased eyes of a drunk?"

"I suppose you need to take things on faith in your line of work."

The old man laughed and finished his drink. "You're probably right. Well, you wanted my advice and I'll give it to you. I believe you, but the police won't. You need to visit Collins in the hospital. The police will have spoken to him already, but I doubt he told them what happened. You must go and hear the truth from him."

"You know," said Jones. "I'll never understand how you read people."

"It's my job. Visit Collins in the hospital and find out what he saw."

"Why would he tell me and not the police?" Jones asked.

"Because you saw it, too. He'll talk because you'll listen. It's not the kind of thing that you can talk to just anyone about. One more cup of coffee?"

"No thanks," Jones said, shaking his head. "I've got to get back to work. It's my lunch break. We've been relocated, and so we all bring in a laptop and sit around a table. They've even got bars over the windows. It's like working in a prison!"

"You have to suffer for your art."

"That's hardly relevant. I make spreadsheets and write proposals. That's not art. If you start to think of art as work, you'll never make a work of art. Will you come with me to see Collins? Not as a priest, but as a friend?"

"Robert, you know I'm here for you. Just give me a call when you need me."

\* \* \*

The hospital smelled of disinfectant and death, and Jones felt ill at ease as he sat beside Montgomery in the waiting room. He watched the priest read a newspaper, looking more like an old man than ever. Montgomery's cassock and collar were gone, replaced by a tweed jacket and corduroy trousers.

Jones twisted his neck to glance at the clock; visitors weren't allowed in until six, and the door was electronically locked. The N.H.S. was efficient – Collins' procedure had already been explained. Although no longer critical, Collins was in the burns unit and strongly sedated. Jones looked at the clock again – three minutes to go. CCTV cameras stared down like evil eyes. Montgomery excused himself and left Jones in morose silence. His ears were assaulted by the harsh buzz of an electronic intercom.

"If you'd care to follow me?" An elderly doctor emerged from nowhere and led Jones to the hospital bed that his colleague now occupied. "If you need anything then give me a shout. I'll be wandering around the ward. You need to be out by seven, so keep an eye on the time and say your goodbyes beforehand."

"Thanks," said Jones.

Collins was lying on his back, and most of his flesh was covered with bandages. Small patches of exposed flesh poked through like snowy volcanoes. He looked like a sunburned mummy, with eyes that stared vacantly around the room. Jones wondered how much morphine was pumping through his system.

"Hi," he said, taking a seat.

The patient said nothing.

Jones moved theatrically and placed a bouquet on the table. "I brought you some flowers."

Collins didn't bat an eyelid – he just kept on staring at his colleague.

"How are you?"

"How am I?" Collins finally croaked, with a broken laugh. It wasn't the bitter, twisted laugh of a man in pain, but the carefree, innocent laugh of a child. To Jones, it sounded sinister.

"Are you all right?" Jones asked.

"I feel amazing." Collins sounded surprised. "But I can't move. Jones, isn't it? Robert?"

"That's me. I was there." Jones lowered his voice and looked around suspiciously. "Do you remember what happened? The accident?"

"I don't."

Jones sighed, regretting a wasted journey.

Then, Collins' eyes lit up with fear. "Wait, I remember! Oh god, how I remember."

His voice was strained, and the pain began to show in his twisted features. His jaw dropped and his eyes flushed.

"What happened?" demanded Jones, bunching his hands into tight fists inside the pockets of his jacket.

"They'll kill me," Collins spluttered, rocking in the hospital bed. A buzzer sounded in the distance, but Jones ignored it. "You don't understand, they'll kill me!"

"Who?" demanded Jones, seething with rising urgency. His determination to uncover the truth was the only thing holding him together. "Who did this to you?"

"You were there," Collins moaned. "You saw them."

The sound of running footsteps echoed through the ward, and Jones felt a doctor at his elbow.

"I'm sorry," the doctor said, drawing a curtain around the bed. "I'm going to have to ask you to leave."

"Who was it?" Jones demanded, fighting to stay at the bedside. "Who did this?"

"Angels," Collins sighed. Then he coughed violently and bawled in agony.

Montgomery was there then, holding Jones' arm and pulling him away. Collins noticed him and screamed like a peasant on the rack.

"Priest!" he cried, writhing desperately on the narrow bed. "I see you, I see your collar and I spit on it!"

A thin thread of saliva flew through the air and struck the priest on the shoulder as the injured man flew into a rage.

"Let's get out of here," murmured Jones, and Montgomery nodded in agreement.

The doctors were struggling to restrain their patient, and the two men made their escape unnoticed. An alarm rang out as they left the building, and all movement stopped. The priest and the businessman said nothing during the long drive home.

# CHAPTER SIXTEEN: A STATEMENT FROM CERN

*Sunday November 22nd, 2009*

**IN A DUSTY BACKROOM** in the old rectory, Father Montgomery settled into an age-worn armchair and sat in silence, illuminated by the light of the ten-inch television. His collar was too tight, and he pulled it off before he choked in the stifling air of the storage room. He should have been preparing his sermons, but the television held more interest. Montgomery smiled, grimly.

The news was full of the usual – death, war, pestilence, and famine. Montgomery had learned enough to know that nothing ever changed. He sometimes wondered whether his career would drive him insane. He spent his days listening to the troubles of a thousand other people, and none of them could listen to his own. He put his feet up and started to watch a confession on a larger scale.

"...and in other news, The European Organisation for Nuclear Research has issued a public statement to unveil the latest results of their experiments."

Montgomery sat up in his hard seat and adjusted the volume, muttering to himself as his old bones creaked in protest.

"Since the official launch of the Large Hadron Collider, the multi-billion pound particle accelerator that's buried under the Franco-Swiss border, CERN's scientists have been busy probing the secrets of the universe."

"Sounds fun," muttered the priest, sipping from his chipped mug.

"Now, in the first public statement of their findings, Senior Co-ordinator Vincent Foster says they've made a major breakthrough."

The journalist disappeared from the screen, and flash photography pushed back the darkness of the rectory. Foster stood behind a podium with a dozen microphones under his tired-looking eyes.

"The Large Hadron Collider was designed to offer new insights into the creation of the universe," Foster began, addressing the scientific community with the pride of a new father. "But we weren't expecting this.

"When we first started our experiments, we faced mistrust and doubt from the general public, and we tried to put a stop to it. The media pounced on unfounded rumours and told us that the world would end, but they couldn't have been further from the truth. Our machine doesn't create black holes, it destroys them."

The priest turned the volume up on the television.

"We believe that dark matter accounts for the vast majority of mass in the observable universe. Inside the LHC, we've unravelled the first clues about its composition. Our studies suggest that DAEMONs are to blame – Dark Electric Matter Objects." Foster leaned closer to the microphone to continue.

"DAEMONs are theoretical, electrically charged, micro black holes. Here in Geneva, we believe that the Large Hadron Collider is capable of destroying them, releasing time, light, and matter back into the universe."

There was a stunned silence from the onlookers; even the photographers kept their fingers away from the shutters.

"Our readings and measurements are completely different to the results that we expected. We're still thinking on our feet, and our top scientists are experimenting and evaluating around the clock. The potential implications of this are limitless. This technology could revolutionise space travel and change the way we view the universe. It could even eliminate the possibility of our solar system's eventual destruction were it to be threatened by a black hole. We expect to publish our amazing results within weeks. Ladies and gentlemen, today has been a wonderful day for science."

The press of the world launched into spontaneous applause, and the BBC reporter acknowledged the end of the article with a smile.

In the rectory, Father Montgomery turned the television off and sat back in his seat, his eyes gleaming thoughtfully in the darkness.

"DAEMONs," he muttered, sounding old and alone. "The God particle. Niall and his Angels…"

As he'd aged, he'd realised that there are always more questions than answers. The Virgin Mary stared down at him from above the sooty fireplace, but he didn't feel her comforting gaze. He fell asleep in his chair in the rectory and didn't wake up until the first rays of the sun were already filtering in through the window.

# CHAPTER SEVENTEEN: THE AFFAIR

*Friday February 2nd, 1962*

**A COOL AIR** blew down from the north, and Father Montgomery coughed and adjusted his tie. After barely two months at the seminary, he already felt uncomfortable without his cassock – he'd always been afraid of the outside world. He checked his pocket watch impulsively, and time moved slowly on. Somewhere in the distance, cars rolled along the main road, almost drowned out by the breeze and the birdsong.

"I hope I'm not too late." Montgomery whirled around, and the creases fell out of his jacket as though they'd never been there.

An enthusiastic smile flickered across his face, to be replaced by a look of sincerity. Sarah looked beautiful – she looked like she'd spent hours on her hair, and the rouge that graced her cheeks removed the stress-lines that their work created. He'd never seen anything so divine.

"You could never be late, I would've waited forever." She giggled and took the arm that he offered with a delicate smile of appreciation. "I'm glad you made it. There were no problems? Nobody saw you?"

"No, I don't think so. I hate all of this secrecy."

"So do I, my love."

They walked through the empty park together, silhouetted by the moon and the stars. They stopped and kissed under an oak tree as the wind whistled through the leaves. Their lips fused together with repressed fury, and their secret passion spread to the world around them. Arm-in-arm, they walked through the twilight, occasionally illuminated by the streetlamps.

"We can't go on like this," she said, clutching him tightly. "It'll kill us. We need to come clean."

Montgomery glanced at her, sadly. "It's not as simple as that, we have the future to think about."

"Life doesn't come with a rulebook, John. We're not breaking any laws. Why can't you think with your heart?"

"Because my head is screaming at me," he muttered, but his words were swallowed by the foliage. He pulled a battered pack of Marlboros from his pocket and lit one, shielding it from the breeze with a frosted palm. "Listen, Sarah..."

"I'm listening."

"I'm sure you are. You don't understand what we're risking here. It doesn't matter whether we're breaking any rules, people see what they want to see, and they want to see a scandal. They'll never allow us to stay, and nowhere else will take us."

"I know more than you think," she whispered, blowing sweet, warm air on his neck. "But I'm prepared to risk everything to be with you."

Montgomery frowned and tried to escape the most difficult decision of his life. "It's too much, Sarah. What if we had children? Can we bring them up in a society that hates them? And our families? Mother is already ill, this could destroy her."

"We'll be careful, John. You'll see. It's different for us."

John Montgomery let his mind and his heart fight it out; his heart won. He grinned, sheepishly, and pulled her closer to him.

"Be a sinner and sin boldly, but believe and rejoice in Christ even more boldly," he quoted. "Martin Luther said that, a Protestant. But perhaps his heart was in the right place."

Tears clouded her eyes like a veil and she kissed his lips and hair, whispering, "Such a martyr."

They made love in the bushes, defying the elements with the fire of young passion. Dead leaves settled in their hair, and the wind whispered around their lustful bodies. Montgomery could see nothing but the distant glow of an electric lamp, and his ears were overwhelmed by the sounds of nature.

They parted in tears and resolved not to meet again, but the damage was already done. The seed of life was buried in Sarah's fertile womb, and their child was on the way. She cried herself to sleep in a state of ambivalence as the moon glided towards the horizon, and Montgomery drained a bottle of whiskey from the comfort of his bed. It stung his eyes and burned his soul, but the pain cleansed the sin and helped him sink into a dreamless sleep.

# CHAPTER EIGHTEEN:
# ANNIHILATION

*Wednesday December 2nd, 2009*

**WITH HIS HEART** beating faster than ever before, Niall stumbled through the streets. The snow was falling like volcanic ash, melting in his hair and clouding his glasses with mist. He stumbled and they fell from his nose, but he was far too terrified to notice. He had no desire to see his adversaries.

The cars whipped past and splashed his legs with muddy water, drenching them to the feeble bone. As his wrinkled feet pounded against the pavement, he felt the shock of the impact through his body – his teeth rattled and ached.

Niall's alcoholic breath cut through the air like a sea mist, and he wobbled unsteadily along the pavement. It was closing time, but he was barred from the local pub for lewd behaviour and a relaxed approach to hygiene. Not that it mattered – he had no money and owned nothing but a ragged coat and the dregs of a bottle of whiskey. The stars stared down disapprovingly, reminding him of childhood dreams that had floated down the drain.

The winter breeze bit his bearded face as he stumbled through the suburbs towards the church. The priest left a storage shed unlocked, and Niall used it as a shelter in the winter months when Montgomery wasn't around to let him into the rectory. He quickened his pace as the rain began to fall, and he froze as a black tomcat dashed in front of him. Its evil eye stared knowingly; Niall chased it in a fury and sent it hissing through an alleyway. He glanced after it.

The only streetlamp flickered and failed, but the alley was flooded with light. The Angels stood beside a cluster of rubbish bins, feasting on the half-light and glowing menacingly from the shadows. Niall dropped his bottle and winced as it smashed on the asphalt; the hypnotic figures turned to face him.

"Man alive," he murmured.

The soles of his heavy shoes thudded against the asphalt as the Angels drifted after him through the side streets. His breaths came in sharp bursts, but he kept a steady pace, and the Angels followed at a distance. From behind a dip in the road, the church crept into view, and he paused for breath before running for the graveyard.

"Why me?" he screamed, with tears pouring from his glassy eyes.

His feet felt the familiar cobblestones of the churchyard, and his hobo-blisters turned the colour of poisoned apples. He made for the relative safety of the shed, slamming the rotten door behind him.

The holy air smelled of mothballs and rusted machinery, and he stared through the dirty window and into the suburban night. The Angels glided down the path towards him, and he felt the cold hands of fear around his collarbone. He searched blindly in the dark for a weapon or a hiding place. He'd seen his pursuers before – he knew what they did and what they wanted.

His wandering hand grasped the cold, metal handle of an old chest freezer, and he resigned himself to his fate. Reluctantly, he struggled to haul himself inside. The light of the Angels shone in the window, and he closed the lid and muttered a hasty prayer. The darkness grew around him.

\*   \*   \*

He was found by the council when the gardening crew scoured the graveyard. The smell of burnt flesh spread through the winter air and into their streaming nostrils. Niall's corpse was charred and crispy, and the dust was disturbed by the dead man's movements. The police were quick to respond, and the chief inspector cast a sour eye over the body.

"Burned to death inside a freezer," he muttered. "Now I've seen everything."

"It won't be long until the press find out." The inspector glanced at his partner, who was stroking his chin in earnest.

"It never is. Fetch the priest."

# CHAPTER NINETEEN: MIXED REPORTS ON CHANNEL FIVE NEWS

*Monday December 7th, 2009*

## NATASHA BLAKE

You never know what to believe, do you? My son told me all about them – he's a theorist, you see. Said they're the latest thing. He watches videos about them online. They're called 'Angels,' and nobody knows how to stop them.

He's always telling me these things and I never pay attention, but then I saw them. They're like moving statues made of light, and they've been following me around for weeks. They stand outside our house at night. You can see them through the curtains like streetlights. All night long they stood there, but I wasn't afraid.

We were getting used to having them around, but that was before they invaded the house. I was just sitting there with my feet up, and they drifted through the walls like ghosts. Of course, I was terrified. There were four of them, standing around the table. And when they talk, it sounds like they're standing in a church, singing a song that only they know the words to.

## HELEN JENNINGS

"We are Angels," they said, and I believed them. My husband was on his knees; I was watching through a crack in the doorway. I thought they were a gang, but I couldn't see any sign of a struggle. I heard the scream, and I knew it was Richard, but what could I do? The police were on their way, and I had no other choice. I had to watch, even if it destroyed me.

They talked to him, about vengeance and retribution. One of them stared at Richard's shirt, and the buttons popped open. With a terrible smile, the tallest stepped forward and pressed his evil hand against my husband's breast. The smell of burnt hair and flesh ripped the world in two, and the screams of the man I loved brought tears to my eyes.

I closed my eyes and listened to Richard's heavy breathing. Then he screamed, a scream that was cut short by the Angels. I ran out the front door and never looked back.

## ERIC HENNEY

"You are a sheep," they said. "And we are the shepherds." Joanna was surrounded by light. It would've been beautiful if she didn't look so scared. That was the last I saw of her. Those so-called 'Angels' knew I was there. They split like an amoeba and chased me down the corridor.

Oscar, our dog, howled like a baby and started pawing at the door. The tallest of the Angels raised a glowing hand. Then, they spoke to me.

"It is not your time," they told me. "We will return for you later, when you least expect it." And then they walked straight through the wall, and I didn't see them again.

As soon as they left, I shook myself and walked towards the living room. I held my breath as I paused with a hand on the door handle; the only sound was Oscar's tragic whimpering. Other than that, it was eerily quiet.

I opened the door to the same old scene, but Joanna wasn't there. She was on the floor beside the fireplace, a seared patch of carpet, and a pyramid of ash, flesh, and burnt bone.

# CHAPTER TWENTY: REBELLION

*Wednesday October 7th, 2009*

**IT HAD BEEN** a bad month. The Andrews didn't understand the change in their daughter – her gentle, loving nature had transformed into near-cruelty, and she was more introverted than ever. Each parent blamed the other as Angelica grew more sadistic by the day.

What about the time they were dragged out of bed at four in the morning to a horrible cacophony of screams? They found their daughter in the kitchen, twisting the cat's tail and giggling at the howls of anguish that it bellowed to the night. Then there was the time that they found her crawling through the garden on her hands and knees, burning insects with a magnifying glass. Something was definitely wrong. "I just don't understand," said Mrs. Andrews, addressing her husband across the kitchen table. "What's wrong with Angelica?"

"Do you want me to have a word with her?"

"What good will that do? You barely know her. Perhaps if you spent less time working and more time with your family, she wouldn't be like this."

"What are you trying to say? If you have something to get off your chest then say it to my face. I can't stand these hints and innuendos."

"I'm saying…" she began, then stopped, glancing at the floral clock on the kitchen wall – 10:27 PM. "Look, you can't pick and choose when to spend time with her."

"I don't need parenting lessons from you."

"Shh!"

A floorboard creaked and they froze. They heard an intake of breath as a shadow passed across the wall, an unevolved burglar with a lurch. The mirage passed in a second, and Ellen Andrews flew up the stairs to gather her daughter in her arms.

"Let me go! You don't own me!" The screaming child swung her puny arms like a pair of sledgehammers.

"Angelica! What's wrong with you?"

The little girl leered like an evil seraph and her mother dropped her to the floor in anguish. For a second, the girl's body hung in the air with a curved spine as though her head and feet were breeze blocks. Then it caught up with gravity and she fell to the ground like a sack of potatoes.

"What's wrong with me?" she rasped. "Oh mother, if you only knew."

# CHAPTER TWENTY-ONE: CONSPIRACY THEORIES FROM NATIONAL NEWSPAPERS

*Wednesday December 9th, 2009*

## ANGELS – THE MYSTERY REVEALED

IT'S THE TERRIFYING phenomenon that's on the tips of tongues across the world, but what exactly *are* Angels? We sent Jerry Jarrell to find out…

I first discovered Angels in Gloucester, when I was researching sources for a story. It was a disappointing interview – my contact was on heavy medication. I was about to leave when he said something that changed my life forever. "Watch out for Angels."

He explained it all – Angels began as a tale told by cautious mothers to their wayward children, a biblical warning. But the fireside tale of original sin and the protectors of Christian virtue is dying out – it's clear that a sinister force is at work.

Nobody knows who or what the Angels are, whether supernatural or frightfully human. They come at night, when our primal DNA sends signals of fear to our tired brains, and they take our loved ones away. But where do these victims go? Some say to horrifying factories, to be processed and packaged and served on the tables of the rich. Others say they're a sinister band of vigilantes, not biblical but scarily real, stamping out hidden perversions wherever they see them.

And they see them everywhere...

## ANGELS MYSTERY GROWS DEEPER

FRESH ALLEGATIONS against local governments have forced the Metropolitan Police to begin an official investigation into the 'Angels' phenomenon.

The number of unexplained disappearances and violent deaths in the London area has risen sharply over the last three months, and local police forces are struggling to deal with the constant bombardment. Police spokesman, Inspector Peter Constance, had this to say:

"We are aware of the situation and believe we have the perpetrators of these crimes within our sights. We would like to reassure the public that we will not falter in our steps to apprehend them. In the meantime, it's of vital importance that we stick together as a community.

"The police force understands how easy it can be to panic in a time of need, but we stress that you should only dial 999 in a genuine emergency. All reports and enquiries can be made by contacting your local police station, either by landline telephone or in person."

It's clear that the Angels epidemic poses a great threat to our society, our safety, and our way of life, like a virus without a cure. As evidence floods in to show similar phenomena in isolated communities across the world, many are turning away from official explanations and asking each other: "What exactly is happening?"

## LIGHT-THIEVES RAID POWER STATION

SECURITY AND STAFF at one of the country's leading power stations were left baffled after a raid by hi-tech burglars.

Employees at Sellafield power station first knew there was a problem when their equipment registered an unusual surge in electricity usage on-site. Shortly afterwards, they saw the first of the intruders, lurking naked in the foyer with no ID. More were soon discovered, and the security team rushed to head them off.

The trespassers forced their way past the officers without a fuss – afterwards, the team reported mixed feelings of horror, repulsion, confusion, and obedience.

"We tried to stop them," said Kevin Naylor, head of security. "But when they told us to do something, we did it. I wouldn't have obeyed my own mother, but we let them pass as though they owned the place."

Once inside the complex, they created a forced power surge, causing no lasting damage but putting the station out of action for forty-eight hours. The intruders haven't been seen since.

If you have any information regarding this incident, don't hesitate to call Sellafield on 08081 570715. Alternatively, file a report at your local police station.

# CHAPTER TWENTY-TWO:
## CONGREGATION

*Thursday December 10th, 2009*

**FATHER MONTGOMERY** was sweating; he was facing the most difficult congregation of his adult career, and he was just as scared as they were. His collar choked him, and he longed to cast it to the floor like an evil spirit. All eyes were on him, and sweat leaked through his pores.

"Good afternoon," he began, stepping into the pulpit with unnatural foreboding. "I'm glad you all could make it."

He surveyed the masses with ambivalence. The priest could tell that they'd been driven to the pews in search of answers, but he had nothing to give them save for empty words and feeble encouragements. They were tired housewives, bachelors with a fear of death, and enthusiastic down-and-outs with nowhere else to be. The stench of desperation was almost overwhelming.

"As you know," he said, starting the sermon. "The country is on fire with rumours of Angels – that's what you're here to learn about. If you're left with any questions, I'll be delighted to answer them at the end.

"So, what are Angels? That's the question it all comes down to, and I suspect that it's the question that brought you here today. If you're expecting an answer then you're wasting your time."

Many of the onlookers shifted guiltily in their seats, but the faithful stayed calm and composed.

"These Angels, from what I understand, are imposters," Montgomery continued. "A modern invention, which mirrors our modern times. We must learn to deal with the threat as a community.

"My advice is simple and personal, as a friend and not a priest. Let us band together to fight them. These Angels, whatever they are, are friends with fear. We must fight them with love and understanding, and that begins at home. Keep in touch with your friends and neighbours, and familiarise yourselves with what to do in an emergency.

"Remember, my friends, that it's a dangerous world. Let us adopt the spirit of the blitz like we did during the war, though attacked by a different enemy. Our doors will always be open, and I'll meet anyone that asks for me. God bless us all in this difficult time."

He was shaking when he descended the wooden steps and left the pulpit, half-afraid and half-alive in the moment. People that he'd never seen before congratulated him and asked questions that he couldn't answer.

"Father?"

He glanced at the pudgy red face of a middle-aged businessman in old tweed.

"What do you think they are, honestly?"

"In a couple of words? Evil incarnate, encouraging darkness and despair. I can't think of anything less angelic."

The businessman looked at him, concern blossoming. "What can we do about it? There must be something."

The priest smiled.

"Of course there is. We can prepare ourselves for the unexpected and go about our lives with love in our hearts." The old priest forced a smile and shook the man by his dry hands, but behind the veil he felt nothing but doubt and foreboding.

# CHAPTER TWENTY-THREE: POSSESSION

*Friday December 11th, 2009*

"**...AND SO** you can see, Father, why we're so worried about Angelica."

Montgomery looked tired, with the weight of the world on his shoulders. His hands grasped absently at the silver cross around his neck.

"I understand your concern," he said, wiping a bead of sweat from his brow and gratefully accepting the tea that was proffered towards him. "And she hasn't acted like this before?"

"Never."

"Well, I'm not sure what I can do. What you're asking of me, it's a lot to think about. I mean, there's no procedure, and I'd have to work outside of the church. We'll have to keep this secret and never speak of it again. If word gets out, it could destroy us all."

"Of course," Mrs. Andrews said, gripping her husband's hand so tightly that he winced and the colour drained from his face. "We won't tell a soul."

"I need to see her again," Montgomery said.

The telephone rang from the study and the semi-present husband rushed to answer it.

His wife sighed and gestured towards the stairs. "As you wish, Father."

The child was sitting up in her bed, leering at the world. Her eyes had a touch of wolfish hunger, and her lips looked like a snake that was rearing to strike. Her arms lay limply at her wasted sides. The Disney duvet was spattered with bodily fluids – vomit, faeces, urine, sweat, saliva, and blood. It looked fresh, and it smelled even fresher.

"You're back, Montgomery." Her voice rasped and grated at the eardrum, and he tried not to look upon her with revulsion.

"I'm here, my child."

"Good, you can tell us about 'original sin'. What does your precious church have to say?"

Her saurian arms crawled across her prepubescent body, and the priest's eyes filled with sorrowful tears. Where her discoloured fingertips touched her virgin skin, purple welts sprung up and formed burst pustules of dead flesh.

"What do you expect me to tell you? The story of the apple and the serpent? The death of Jesus Christ, the son of God? The entire Bible is a lesson in sin, how do you expect me to condense it?" He struggled to look at the child with love, to force his mind away from the bias of his senses. His instincts told him that the monster must be destroyed, but his educated brain was pleading for him to see sense.

"I don't know," she said, stretching as much as her chains would allow her. "Tell us how you live with yourself, how you sleep at night with the knowledge that you're fed on a daily basis. You're nothing but a filter for sin and depravity, and you see it everywhere. You permit people to share their poisonous secrets so they can leave feeling innocent, then watch as they go out and commit the same acts all over again."

"Someone has to do it," he replied, picking his way through the verbal trap. "Why not me?"

The apparition in the bed just laughed, and the priest wondered what he was up against.

"We will say nothing more. Next time we meet, it will be upon the battlefield." The wasted child lay back in its bed and began to vomit a fresh load of acrid bile on to the dirty silk.

The Father crossed himself and patted his breast – the old heirloom was still there, the musty Bible that first introduced him to his maker.

Outside, the fretful mother pulled the priest aside, offering tea and whiskey to steady his nerves. He accepted both and sank into an armchair, heavy with the contagious stench of depression.

"So what do you think, Father? Can you help us?" The priest said nothing and led the way towards the front door.

On the doorstep, he pulled a cigarette from a battered packet and raised it to his shaking lips. His old fingers looked like white candles as they cupped the flame of a matchstick.

"I'll be in touch," he said, disappearing into the unyielding night.

# CHAPTER TWENTY-FOUR:
# VISITATION

*Saturday December 12th, 2009*

**THE SWEAT WAS DRIPPING** from Jones' brow in a localised rain as he reached the top of the stairs and began to fiddle with his keys. It had been a long, relentless day.

It started off normally enough – a single slice of lukewarm toast and a glass of off-coloured water. The inner-city traffic was unforgiving and dreary, and the hours in the office were long, cold, and boring. Now he was back at home, and something didn't feel right.

The winter chill seeped through the double-glazing and into his bones, so he turned up the heat and wrapped himself in a heavy coat. He could hear the icy wind blowing through the eaves of the old apartment, and for a crazy second he longed to be outside with the harsh teeth of winter gnawing at his naked flesh. He strolled over to the bay windows, threw the curtains open, and looked outside.

"We have been waiting for you." The dreadful voice appeared from nowhere and seemed to shake the building.

Outside, suspended in mid-air like eerie Russian dolls, a trio of Angels radiated light. Jones already knew enough. His first instinct was to draw the curtain and call the police, but he knew it was useless.

Instead, he stood tall and shouted through the thick glass. "What do you want from me?"

Their faces remained impassive, but he could sense that they could hear him. Understanding sparked in the air like electricity on overhead wires.

"We want you to tell us about your nightmares."

Jones laughed nervously and patted desperately at his pockets. The Angels seemed unconcerned. His handset flickered into life, and his speed-dial kicked in; a couple of miles away, in the back room of Montgomery's dilapidated church, an answering machine started rolling.

"I don't have nightmares," he said, carefully. "I have dreams. Why don't you help me out here?"

"We are not here to help, we are here to judge." As one, the Angels floated through the moonlight towards the window. The air shimmered like a mirage; after a second of impossibility, they were through the glass and inside the apartment. "Feed us, tell us a story."

"I'm not telling you anything," Jones said. The terror was beginning to leave him. *Enough is enough,* he thought. *It's time for someone to take a stand.* "Go back to hell."

"What makes you think that hell exists?"

"You exist," he replied. "And that's enough proof for me."

For almost a minute, they stared at each other like wild animals preparing to fight. Jones was shaking with adrenaline; he blinked and broke the silence.

"If you leave right now, nobody needs to know that you were here," he said.

"If you satisfy our hunger, we will leave."

Jones looked at them, thoughtfully.

"Can I trust you?" he asked. They nodded, but he still felt uneasy. "All right, I'll do it."

Jones turned his back on them for long enough to pour a scotch on the rocks; when he turned around, they were still staring at him with their proud wings folded behind their backs.

They looked... hungrier.

"Tell us everything... those dirty little secrets. Tell us about what you did with Pam in the photocopier room, or about the time that you pushed an old woman over in your rush to make it to work on time."

Jones frowned at them – he'd never mentioned that to anybody.

"I didn't even stop to pick her up. What can I tell you that you don't already know?"

"How did it feel? What went through your head? Time is not important to us." They stood there like impassive statues outside an ancient castle, barring the way for strangers.

And so Jones talked and talked until he thought he could talk no longer. He told them about the pride he'd felt during the birth of his son, and his subsequent inability to be a 'real' father. He told them about his ruthless streak, about the way he used to squash bugs as a child because he wanted to feel the power of life and death over something, anything. And he told them about the way that sometimes, at the bottom of the bottle of scotch when it was too late to be the night before and too early to be the day after, he sometimes thought about ending it all, until the first rays of dawn sent him to bed for a couple hours of troubled sleep.

But there was only so much to say, and Jones was tired, and he started to babble incoherently. It was something about someone long ago, and he couldn't remember whether he'd slept with her or not. They started to press in closer and closer, until he was ready to give up and hand himself over.

Then the doorbell rang and they scattered like dust in a hurricane. Jones remained where he was for a couple of seconds to give his lagging brain a chance to catch up before he opened the door.

"Good evening," said Father Montgomery. "I picked up your message and came over as soon as I could. It sounded like something was wrong."

Jones smiled and invited the old man inside.

"It's an evil night," he said, standing aside to allow the dripping priest into the hallway. He took Montgomery's jacket and hung it from the coat-rack with shaking hands. The priest could see that something was terribly wrong, and the concern dampened his wise, old eyes. Jones poured out two measures of Bell's and handed one of the glasses to Montgomery.

"So what happened?" Montgomery asked.

Jones stared at the floor, saying nothing while he allowed his thoughts to form. At last, he sat down, gestured for Montgomery to do the same, and drained his glass. "They were here, Father," he said. "The Angels."

The priest's face flushed with interest and he leaned forward in his chair. "They were? What did they want?"

"I don't know," Jones said. "But I'm sure they'll be back."

"What makes you so sure?"

"You weren't here, Father. They didn't look like they'd go away and forget about me. I doubt they've ever forgotten anything." Jones pulled himself to his weary feet and strolled over to the window. An early morning fog shrouded the city in a misty jacket, and the temperature was beginning to drop. "Help me, John. I just don't know what to do anymore."

"I'll tell you what we'll do," Montgomery said. He spoke with the voice of reason – calm and controlled in a world of confusion, like a midwife at a birth. "We'll wait for them, together. If they are what they say they are, I'd like a word."

# CHAPTER TWENTY-FIVE: EXORCISM

*Sunday December 13th, 2009*

"**THANK YOU** for coming, Father."

Montgomery looked tired and worn; his aged face needed ironing. He smiled, thinly.

"The pleasure is all mine, Mrs. Andrews. The Lord has blessed our meeting. Now let us hope that he blesses your daughter. Is she upstairs?"

"Yes. You'll find her where you left her, although I should warn you… she's grown worse. A lot worse." She stifled a sob as her husband wrapped a tender arm around her heaving shoulders. "Do you want to go and see her?"

"I'll do just that, but I need to prepare before I go in there. May I use your bathroom?"

"Of course."

"Thank you," Montgomery said. "Perhaps you should take this time to visit your daughter. This will be a stressful experience for her. Does anyone know that I'm here?"

"No, Father. We've kept the whole affair a secret. It's not something to tell the neighbours."

"Good," he replied. "That's how it should be. You understand, I'm here as a friend and not a priest, but I'll do what good I can."

"Yes, Father," Mrs. Andrews replied. "I understand. But we have to try!"

Montgomery smiled and excused himself, before locking himself in the bathroom. He caressed the simple crucifix that he carried – a gift from *her* – and tried to decide what to do. Sighing, he pulled two vials from his briefcase; one was full of 'holy' water, prepared on the sacred grounds of the church, and the other was empty. With exaggerated care, he filled the empty vial at the bathroom sink, replaced the stopper, and dried it on a towel. Then he said a short prayer, gathered his thoughts and belongings, and climbed the stairs to the young girl's room.

As soon as he opened the door, his nostrils were assaulted by the stench – it was like a glue-boiling vomit factory. The possessed lay comatose in her bed, her skin scabbed and raw. A cold wind blew through the open window and slammed the door behind him; the apparition in the bed sat bolt upright.

"So," it said. "You came."

The child's voice was unholy – it grated at the ears and reverberated inside the skull, like the death howl of a dozen people.

"Of course," he replied. "We have unfinished business. What are you?"

"What do your eyes tell you?"

The priest ignored the question and began to unpack his suitcase – a Bible, a bell, and a candle. He muttered a short prayer and turned towards the girl.

"My eyes tell me that your heart has stopped and that you're no longer breathing, but my mind says that's impossible."

The child leered at him.

"May I check your pulse?" he asked.

"I won't stop you," she replied.

The priest didn't trust her, but he reminded himself that she was just a child and bent down beside her with his eyes on hers. They were jaundiced and reptilian, like something from a comic book or a horror film. He pressed her wrist, looking for an elusive pulse, but he quickly pulled away – her skin was so hot that his fingertips burned and sizzled.

"What are you?" he gasped, horror-struck.

The creature laughed. "Surely you recognise us, Father. Are you not a priest?"

"I am," he said.

"And we are Angels."

He nodded; he'd had his suspicions.

"You've heard of us?"

"As a rumour," he replied. "But why are you here? And what do you want?"

"We want to see sins. We feed on them like you feed on the planet. We will not rest until we feast on all of the corruption in this wicked world."

"And a child is corrupt?" Montgomery asked. It bared its teeth at the priest, little chunks of calcified tissue set in foul, rotten gums.

"Do you not remember your childhood, priest? Corruption is forced upon you before you even leave the womb. Your people are conceived in sin, born in shame to an ugly world, fed with processed food that's bought with dirty money. You lie, you cheat, you steal. You kill animals and insects for food and fun. You lust after others, have pornography force-fed to you by the media, gossip about death, war, pestilence, and famine, then die alone with the knowledge of secret sins that will never be discovered. Do you want us to continue?"

"Some would argue that we don't have a choice," the priest replied.

"Perhaps. But that doesn't concern us."

In silence, Montgomery reached into his case and withdrew the vial of tap water. The creature in the bed looked unconcerned.

"Do you know what this is?" he asked.

There was no response.

"This is holy water, blessed by the Lord."

Without warning, Montgomery removed the stopper and threw the water at the demon in the bed. It sizzled and boiled on the skin, but the creature barely reacted. He sighed; then without warning, he threw the contents of the second vial towards her. She frowned at him.

"We know what you are trying to do," she said. "If you wanted us to leave, you should have asked."

The light of intelligence disappeared from the child's eyes as she slumped forwards in her bed. The priest dashed to catch her, but he recoiled at the touch of her skin – ice cold and clammy, like a corpse. Without hope, he checked for a pulse – there was nothing.

The outcome was written in his eyes when he climbed reluctantly down the stairs towards the dining room. The parents looked up expectantly – Father Montgomery lowered his eyes to the floor.

"Your daughter is… with God now," he said.

"What are you telling us?" screamed Mrs. Andrews. Tears clouded the beautiful eyes that looked so much like her daughter's. Her husband dragged the old priest to the door.

"You did your best," he said. "We expected nothing more from you. Now go, no-one must ever know that you were here."

The door slammed shut in his face; the priest looked up through the night at the girl's bedroom window. Cursing to himself, he picked up his briefcase and walked away.

# CHAPTER TWENTY-SIX: THE PLAN

*Monday December 14th, 2009*

**FATHER MONTGOMERY** and Robert Jones sat in silence at a table in Jones' apartment. They talked, made notes, drank endless cups of tea, and asked questions that neither of them could answer, then arrived at the conclusion that something must be done. "I have a theory," said the priest, breaking a half hour of silence. "Although I have no evidence to support it, and I can't pretend I understand the science."

"I'm listening," Jones replied.

"Well, I've been thinking… do you remember the furore at CERN? You know, the black hole scandal?"

"I remember," said Jones. "The media said the world would end, that CERN's machine could create black holes. We watched the coverage at work. But what does that have to do with Angels?"

"From what we understand," Montgomery began. "From what they've told us and from what our eyes make us believe, they're made entirely of light. Conscious light, but still light. The rumours got it backwards. CERN's machine destroys black holes instead of creating them." The old priest's eyes were aglow with passion.

Jones imagined Montgomery as an artist or musician. The same sense of urgent creativity surrounded him, little thunderclouds of thought. "Is that possible?" he asked.

"It's... theoretically possible," Montgomery replied. "Look at Newton's third law. Every action has an equal and opposite reaction. If it's possible to create a black hole, should it not be possible to destroy one? Besides, I saw it on the television. CERN practically confirmed it."

"It makes sense," conceded Jones with a shrug.

"Now if that were the case, that would explain a lot," continued the priest, oblivious to anything outside his technological sermon. "Black holes swallow light and compress it. Perhaps that's where the Angels were, trapped in hibernation. And if black holes were destroyed, the light could spill back out into the universe."

The priest took a sip of his drink and closed his tired eyes. Jones' head still whirred, but he was a product of the times – he had to see proof before he supported a theory.

"That assumes they're really made out of light," Jones said. "Which seems like quite the assumption."

"Tell me..." Montgomery sighed. "You've seen them, you've talked to them. Do you believe they're made of light?"

"Yes," Jones replied.

"So do I."

They exchanged glances, and Jones felt his mouth go dry.

"Do you understand what that means?" Montgomery asked. "This is huge; we need to get to the bottom of it."

"Agreed, but where do we start? We know next to nothing."

The old man smiled, enigmatically. "I suggest we start at CERN. Perhaps they know something, although they won't be happy to speak to us. We must keep our eyes and ears open, follow up on every lead, and find out as much about the Angels as we can. They seem to be an enemy of yours, and so they're also an enemy of mine."

Jones looked up at him, in awe. "You've really thought things through, haven't you?" he asked.

"Of course," Montgomery replied. "You realise that the steps we're taking are unprecedented? We're about to leap off the diving board and into the unknown. We can't know what to expect, but it could be dangerous. If the Angels are what they say they are, victory may be impossible. I hope you realise that."

"I understand."

They lapsed into silence again; then Jones stood up and put the kettle on.

"This is real," he said. "Isn't it?"

The priest nodded, morosely. "If only it weren't."

# CHAPTER TWENTY-SEVEN: CERN

*Wednesday December 16th, 2009*

**THE COMMERCIAL JET** glided noisily through the sky, battered by the storm that assaulted the city. Thousands of metres below, Geneva was witnessing its worst weather of the year.

"Are you ready?" asked Jones, looking carefully at his friend and companion.

The priest was reclining beside him, with one eye closed and the other eye focused on the window. "We'll land soon, there's no going back after this. Are you sure you want to do this?"

"Of course I am. I'm as ready as I'll ever be. You can hardly prepare for the unexpected."

The aeroplane made a shaky final descent, and the travellers finally disembarked and made their way through passport control.

"Let's grab our cases and find the hotel," Montgomery said. "We can plan our next move from there."

It felt strange to be among ordinary people with such an unnatural goal, but snatches of foreign conversation and childish laughter were alien enough to remind them of their mission. Their bags were quick off the carousel – they were travelling light and only half-expecting to return. Jones and Montgomery were soon on their way to the hotel, gliding stylishly through the streets of Geneva in the back of a bright yellow taxi. When they arrived, a guest was waiting.

"Mr. Blaise Atkins," said the receptionist, introducing them to a middle-aged man with designer stubble and expensive glasses. "He said he had an appointment to see you."

"Ah!" exclaimed Montgomery, shaking their visitor's hand excitedly. "So pleased to meet you, we've heard a lot about you."

"The pleasure is all mine," Atkins said, with an accent that was so bizarre, Montgomery couldn't place it. "I hear that you have some important questions for me. Is there anywhere private we can go?"

"There's our room, once we get the keys. I'm sorry we're not prepared. We weren't expecting to see you until tomorrow. We've only just arrived," Montgomery explained, gesturing towards his luggage with an expressive sweep of the arm.

"I know, but this can't wait," Atkins replied, lowering his voice. "No-one knows that I'm here, and certainly no-one official. I could lose my job. You understand, gentlemen, that this conversation isn't happening?"

"Ah," said Jones. "It's one of those meetings. We'll see what we can do. Perhaps we can hijack the lounge."

But the lounge was busy, and so they waited in silence to be shown up to their room; the concierge arrived ten minutes later and pointed them to room 108. Atkins looked cautiously around to inspect for potential bugs, while Montgomery brewed a pot of coffee to be served in plastic teacups.

"So," Montgomery said. "We're all ears. What is it that you have to tell us?"

"Let me explain why I'm here. You see, Father Montgomery, everyone who worked on the project was sworn to secrecy, an oath that I had every intention of keeping. But I was having a crisis and needed someone to talk to, and then you called my office. A priest, asking questions that I'm not allowed to answer," Atkins laughed. "But I'm here now, and you will hear my confession.

"As you somehow seem to know, the troubles with the Angels are linked to the Collider that's buried beneath the border. I was there when we turned it on, our moment of glory before the trouble started. Everything was running smoothly until we began the first collisions."

"Your first attempts at discovering the God particle," murmured Montgomery, thoughtfully.

"Correct," Atkins replied. "At first, we were just confused by some unexpected readings. Light inside the Collider and unexplained energy surges. We investigated, but we didn't know whether they were the results that we were looking for or something else entirely. I mean, we're on the cutting edge of physics. Half of the time we make it up as we go along. Oh yes, it looks neat and tidy from the outside, but you should see the chaos behind the theory. Do you know how terrifying it is to be testing something that could blow the scientific world apart?"

"I don't," admitted Jones. "But I know what it feels like when two irreconcilable truths collide, and I imagine it's roughly the same."

"That's one way of putting it," Atkins agreed. "It's hard to explain. Strange things have been happening, and things have gone missing. People said the LHC was haunted, and it wasn't hard to believe it. Then the 'accidents' started. Old Josef had a heart-attack, and when they found him, he looked ungodly. You know *The Scream*?"

"The painting?"

"The very same," replied Atkins. "He looked like that, only worse. Then there was Nikolas, a veteran cyclist and boxer. They found him burned in a rubbish bin, with his ribcage broken in two. There aren't many people who could've done that."

"So you don't think it was a person?" asked Jones. The scientist gave him a look that he couldn't understand, and Montgomery waited patiently for the story to continue.

"You could be right. Who can tell? Shortly after that, the rumours of avenging Angels began to surface. Kolinsky swore that he'd seen them, but we didn't believe him. A week later, he was killed in a car crash. They said that he swerved to avoid something and lost control of the vehicle."

"That sounds suspicious," Montgomery observed.

"It was. They found no sign of another vehicle. But was it really caused by Angels? I'm a man of science. I rarely take things on faith. But if these Angels do exist, and if they're really made of light, your theory is plausible. It's logical, but can science prove it? Perhaps only time will tell."

"I'm a man of faith," said Montgomery. "If you tell me that it's possible, then I can do the rest."

"It's possible," Atkins replied. "Though perhaps unlikely. But it's the only theory we have, the only thing that explains everything that's happened since the launch of the Collider. I'll try to dedicate some time to it, but you have to understand that there's not much I can do."

"Of course," the priest replied.

The scientist fiddled with his mobile phone and began to climb from his seat. "I really must be going. Thank you for agreeing to meet me. Need I remind you that this conversation never happened? That we've never corresponded?"

"Our lips are sealed," replied Jones.

They bade a hasty farewell in the snowy garden, and priest and scientist met each other's eyes as they exchanged a firm handshake. Then Atkins disappeared into the afternoon as Jones and Montgomery retired to their hotel room in silence. At last, they sat down to share a strong drink.

"Well," said Jones. "I think that went pretty well."

Montgomery looked over with the hint of a smile. "What did?"

# CHAPTER TWENTY-EIGHT:
## VENGEANCE

*Thursday December 17th, 2009*

**BLAISE ATKINS SIGHED** and licked his lips, turning the pages of a dirty textbook. There was nothing, no record of any experiment in the history of scientific exploration that could prove or disprove the priest's theory. It was like trying to catch a ghost or to vaccinate against bad luck. The task was made harder because he couldn't leave a paper trail, and he didn't even know what he was looking for.

The telephone at his desk began to ring, and in the cold stillness of the dark laboratory, he hesitated before answering. The receiver felt cold against his ear as he answered in broken French. There was no response, just angry static and silence.

"Damn kids," he muttered.

The nuisance calls were getting worse; almost every evening, he went home to the same message – shrill wails and screams, the threatening buzz of static electricity and lost signals. He coughed and turned another page, then sat back in his chair and listened to the silence. He heard nothing but the subtle gleam of waiting machinery and the fans of a thousand computers.

His eyes flicked back to the scientific bible that lay open on the table in front of him, but there was nothing, no overlooked paragraph or new experiment that could help him. Nobody knew what was happening, and it terrified him. He sighed and closed the book, then turned around. He wasn't alone.

"Mr. Atkins." The dreadful voices echoed through the underground complex in a hellish choir, and adrenaline rushed through the scientist like a drunken matador. "We're pleased to meet you, at last."

His eyes widened as he took his adversaries in. "Who are you?" His voice was cold and afraid, but it had an excited edge to it.

"You already know what we are," they said.

The harsh electric lighting seemed to bounce off their skin and into his head like a bullet, and he had to shade his eyes from the glare.

There were half a dozen of them, shimmering and blurring together so he couldn't count their number. They were naked, but they were naked like statues; their faces wore terrible expressions of neutrality, like Mafia hitmen – never scared or intimidated, always ready to kill.

"You're right," he said, rising from his chair. "I know what you are, all right. But I don't know why you're here."

The Angels watched him impassively – there was nowhere for him to go; they were blocking the only exit, and the lab was like a labyrinth. Hundreds of metres below them, the Large Hadron Collider throbbed and hummed like a caged lion.

"You are not meant to understand. It is enough that we understand, and we do."

"You're really real, then," he muttered.

They ignored him. "All will be judged."

The statement fell like light through a widow's veil, and the scientist shrank back in awe. He was pressed against the desk now, and the Angels' united voice was growing louder and more powerful by the second.

"Kneel before us if you dare to confess your sins."

"I'm a scientist," he said, trying to edge along the desk and away from them. "Why should I discuss religion with a possible delusion?"

They weren't coming any closer, but the strange light that illuminated them was growing more defined. He could feel the heat from their skin, an intense glow that made sweat leak through him like morning dew.

"Because you have no choice. You will feed us or you will die." The leading Angels took a step forward, and the uncomfortable heat grew hotter. It felt like he was trapped beneath the surface of a hot bath.

"And after I 'feed you'?" Atkins said. "There's nothing to stop you from killing me. If you're going to kill me, kill me now and let me die with dignity."

"And spoil our fun? Mr. Atkins, we are only just beginning. We will have you begging for mercy, screaming every evil deed and indecent act you've ever committed. Your eyes will bleed tears of resentment towards the world, and then you will die, when our hunger is satisfied." They inched closer to the scientist, and the discomfort grew into pain.

"What can I tell you?" he moaned. "I'm no different to anyone else. What have I done that's so terrible?"

"All will be judged. Feed us."

"When I was ten, I stole my sister's bike and rode all of the way to the city," Atkins began. "I sold it and spent the money on chocolate. I ate so much that I couldn't walk home, and my parents had to come and collect me."

"Is that the best that you can do?" The Angels took another step closer and the air grew polluted with burnt hair and singed flesh. "A childish misdemeanour, nothing more. We want something deeper, more sinful."

The scientist whimpered in near-convulsive pain.

"I've been cheating on my wife with one of the apprentices."

"Tell us more. Why did you do it? How did it feel?"

"Terrible," he wailed. "And yet, so right. You can't know how frustrating it is to be trapped in a loveless marriage. Even my children hate me. They say I spend too much time at work. No-one understands me. Claudia is different, she knows how I feel."

The Angels seemed appeased, but it was temporary. Atkins felt as though he'd thrown a child to a pack of hungry wolves, giving them a taste for soft flesh and brittle bones.

"It's not enough," they said. "We need more."

The scientist whimpered again and played his last, desperate card.

"I killed someone!" he shouted. "When I was nineteen, in a fight over a girl. I hit him, and he went down like a bag of bricks. He never got back up. I didn't even hit him that hard, he just…" Atkins trailed off as the Angels' faces grew lined with anger and disgust.

"We hate the taste of lies, Mr. Atkins," they said, edging closer as he cowered behind his blistered hands, moaning in white hot agony. "Prepare to pay for your sins."

The Angels laughed with the timbre of a dozen harps, then rushed towards him in a river of light that washed over him. The last thing that the defeated scientist saw was their impassive faces, still hungry under the harsh electric glare. Then a calm breeze took his mind away, and the Angels glided through the ceiling and left the scalded body to fester and decay.

# CHAPTER TWENTY-NINE:
# MONTGOMERY'S VOICEMAIL
# MESSAGE

*Friday December 18th, 2009*

**"HELLO,** you're through to Father John Montgomery. Unfortunately, I'm not available to take your call at the moment, but if you'd like to leave your name, telephone number, and a brief message, I'll get back to you as soon as I can. Please speak clearly after the tone."

BEEP.

"It's Jones. Father, it's all over the newspapers – have you seen it? 'CERN scientist found dead inside laboratory.' They're saying he was burned to death – check this out, they released a statement.

"'We are sad to confirm the death of Professor Blaise Atkins inside the CERN laboratory on Friday night. Although, as a key member of our scientific team, he had access to his workstation at all hours, he wasn't on active duty at the time of his death. We're urging anyone with relevant information to come forward. We intend to co-operate fully with any police investigation.'

"What do you make of that, then? We need to meet up again as soon as possible, something's definitely going on here. Call me, okay? I'm worried. More worried than ever."

# CHAPTER THIRTY: THE MEETING

*Friday December 18th, 2009*

**FATHER MONTGOMERY** didn't look up from the book he was reading.

"Don't bother knocking," he said, turning the discoloured pages of his Bible and running his finger across the verses. "Are you familiar with Psalm 23?"

The Angels nodded cautiously; the priest still had his back to them. He found his place and began to read to the spectral audience.

"The Lord is my shepherd, I shall not want. He makes me lie down in green pastures. He leads me beside still waters. He restores my soul. He leads me in paths of righteousness for his name's sake. Even though I walk through the valley of the shadow of death, I will fear no evil, for you are with me; your rod and your staff, they comfort me. You prepare a table before me in the presence of my enemies; you anoint my head with oil; my cup overflows. Surely goodness and mercy shall follow me all the days of my life, and I shall dwell in the house of the Lord forever." Slowly, the priest turned around in his chair.

"Very good," chorused the Angels. "But how much of that do you really believe? We've seen inside you, we've seen the wound that your faith left behind. Tell us, how long have you lived in hypocrisy?"

The priest frowned for a moment, then smiled, sadly. "For far too long. But God is benevolent, and he'll forgive me."

"Is he, now?" Their aquiline faces flickered, and the priest saw anger and laughter. "You believe that God created all life. Does that include us? On the eighth day, he said 'let there be ruin,' and we were born of light and released into the universe."

"May I ask a question?" Montgomery said. "From one theist to another?"

"If we can refuse to answer."

The priest smiled again; in the old leather armchair, he looked beaten and worn.

"Why me?" he asked. "Why quiz a tired old man about his faith? There must be other priests that can offer more information."

"We like the taste of your sins."

He made no attempt to plead purity – instead, he looked them one-by-one in their cold, heartless eyes.

"I see," he said. "And are you what you say you are? Are you made of light or flesh? Do you have skin like I do?"

"Both," they answered. "And more."

"But how?" Montgomery asked. "Your existence is impossible."

"Perhaps to you. We don't concern ourselves with such mundane matters. We think, therefore we are. What else is there? We are not weak like you. We do not need love, we do not need religion. We do not feel hatred, we do not need rest or comfort."

"Then what do you need?"

For a moment, there was silence – not even the whispering of the traffic penetrated the invisible curtain. Then, with the mounting awareness of an un-scratchable itch, reality came back, and the Angels spoke again.

"We need secrets," they explained. "Dark secrets to keep us nourished through the aeons. And that is why we need you." The lines on their faces seemed to soften, and the priest's concentration failed. For a split second, they looked almost human. "You could tell us everything; you have heard it all before."

"I'll tell you nothing," he growled. "My secrets are my own and that's how they'll stay."

"Do you take confessional?"

"Everything I hear is God's secret," Montgomery said. "I'm just the arbiter of his message."

There was a sudden noise from the road outside the church's gates, and the Angels pressed together. Montgomery noticed and smiled – whatever they were, whatever they wanted, they were on enemy territory. The grounds of the church were intimidating even to the priest, but he knew that as long as he stood there, they couldn't touch him. One by one, they faded into the night. There was only the leader left, glowing like a terrible nightlight.

"We will meet again," he screeched. "I will ensure it."

Without his brothers beside him, he sounded like a piano falling from a window. The priest shrank back into his seat as the demonic vocal chords unfolded to bellow their infernal sentence.

The Angel disappeared, and the priest closed his eyes, confused and exhausted. Dark thoughts clouded his mind, and he sank into an uneasy sleep. He woke to a friendly face and a soft pair of hands; Jones wafted the scent of slow-roasted coffee under his nostrils.

"I heard voices," he said, as the befuddled priest drank and warmed his hands on the cup. "Are you all right?"

Montgomery grinned like a teenager with a plan.

"I'm fine," he said. "I have an answer to a question that's been bothering me for months."

"You do?" asked Jones. "And what's that?"

"The Angels. They really do exist. We need to decide on our next move, before they decide on theirs."

# CHAPTER THIRTY-ONE: THE WORLD STANDS STILL

*Saturday December 19th, 2009*

"**OUR TOP STORY** tonight... the underground crime wave continues to spread, with reports of Angels in Peru, Madagascar, North Korea, and Jamaica.

"Police forces across the world are baffled, adding their consternation to the confusion of top criminologists, theists, and scientists alike. Disappearances are on the rise, the rate of violent deaths is at an all-time high, and government officials have nothing new to say.

"The British public can rest assured that we're doing everything we can to crack down on the perpetrators of these crimes. We've made over a thousand arrests in the London area alone, and we ask for your continued co-operation in this time of need. If you see anything suspicious, we urge you to call our information hotline – 08081 570211. We're also working closely with foreign governments to put an end to this international crime wave.

"But will that be enough? Experts warn of a worldwide pandemic of revenge crimes and vigilantism. Police have stressed the importance of leaving peace-keeping to the professionals and of calling the emergency services only in the case of a genuine emergency.

"One thing is certain… this can't go on forever. Perhaps the Christmas spirit will convince the Angels, whoever they may be, to rethink their strategy of fear and terror. Let's hope that the season of goodwill wins them over. Back to you, Clive."

# CHAPTER THIRTY-TWO: RESEARCH

*Monday December 21st, 2009*

**THE FLOOR WAS COLD** and unloving; Jones had had a rough night's sleep, waking every time a distant gust of wind howled in the eaves like the ghost of a long-dead child in the rafters. The winter chill bit him as he tossed and turned, but from the camp-bed beside him, Father Montgomery breathed deeply and serenely. Only a couple of days earlier, they'd been in Geneva. It had been a productive trip, until Jones heard about the death of Vincent Foster. They'd hopped on the first plane home.

Jones sighed and rolled over as the mist began to fade and the morning sun crept over the horizon, bringing warmth and the promise of a new day. Outside the church, a dog barked twice and was cut suddenly short, and Jones' tired eyes were watering. He rubbed them unconsciously and fell asleep.

He woke up to the shrill sound of a Nokia ringtone reverberating through the eaves. Jones fumbled through his pockets, looking for the handset, and pulled it reluctantly to his ear.

"What?" he grumbled.

The words that came out of the tiny speakers were angry and urgent. "Jones, where the hell are you? You haven't been at the office for a week, and we need you. We're pitching tomorrow, have you forgotten?"

"No," he replied. "I haven't."

"Get in here right now," his manager demanded. "Or you're fired."

Jones could almost feel the spittle travelling across the airwaves.

"You can't fire me, I quit. Some things are more important than your money." For a second, the line was silent except for the faint crackle of interference.

"Are you sure about this?"

"You heard me," Jones said, dropping the call and switching his phone to silent.

Beside him, the old priest stirred and mumbled something about brimstone and betrayal. Jones leant over him and stroked his sweaty cheeks.

"Rest," he whispered, soothingly. "We've got a long day ahead of us."

\*   \*   \*

Jones' day had been wasted with fruitless Googling while Montgomery went about his duties. The web was just that, strings of relevant but useless articles pointing to a central evil, the Angels. Every time his brain started to tire, he stepped outside for a breath of fresh air.

Jones smoked his seventh cigarette of the day as he watched the sun go down on the estate behind the church. A cough behind him signalled the entrance of the priest, but Jones finished his cigarette in silence before turning round to address Montgomery.

"I lost my job," said Jones.

"I thought as much. You don't need it anymore."

"And I thought you gave good advice."

"My friend," said Montgomery, patting him on the back. "You won't need a job where we're going. There are two possible destinations... we die and so does humanity, or we live and you spend your days on national news and talk shows."

Jones shuddered and lit another cigarette. "You're sure there's not a third?"

*　*　*

Later that night, when Jones relented and fell asleep on the only bed in the rectory, Montgomery finished his Hail Marys and walked over to the window. The dull dormitory was like a jail cell, and the winter chill swept through the dusty rectory like a famine.

Outside, the graveyard was deserted, and the moon shone through the pollution like a lighthouse. Then it dipped behind a cloud and was gone. Montgomery was not alone.

In the distance, a flash of light beamed from the dark sky and earthed itself on the roof of an office block. A wisp of smoke rose towards the heavens and evaporated; then, a half-dozen Angels materialised. Montgomery stared at them over the top of his long nose. They stared right back at him.

# CHAPTER THIRTY-THREE: THE END IS NIGH

*Tuesday December 22nd, 2009*

**EARLY THE FOLLOWING MORNING,** Jones rose from a light slumber to a misty grey morning that seemed to shroud everything in mystery. Reluctantly, he dragged himself into the bathroom to wash and shave, knowing that no-one was going to see him. He sensed another wasted day at the computer.

The razorblade was sharper than expected, and as he dragged it across his skin, he nicked an old cut and blood began to drop into the basin. Each drop sounded like the tolling of a bell, and Jones watched it impassively as it rolled slowly down the drain. When he'd finished, he dabbed the wound with toilet paper until the blood began to coagulate.

\* \* \*

The church was deserted, and Father Montgomery was still asleep on the floor of the rectory. Jones glanced at his peaceful face and left him to get some rest, walking down the aisle and out through the heavy oaken doors.

He looked left and then right; the sun's early light washed over him like a cold shower. Jones felt dirty – he hadn't bathed properly for several days. A lick of wind blew dust and dirt across the graveyard and stained the legs of his trousers. He heard the faraway bark of a stray dog and shivered.

Jones lit the last of his cigarettes and stepped away from the door of the church, strolling through the yard in the half-light. He could hear something, a distant whisper like the spray of an aerosol. He followed his ears along the beaten path, examining the abutments for the source of the strange noise. He saw the boy a moment later.

"Hey!" he shouted, raising a finger and pointing at the miscreant.

A teenage boy in skater shoes was clutching a can of spray-paint. His peaked cap faced backwards and his jeans sagged, exposing an inch of boxer shorts beneath his t-shirt. He ignored Jones completely and continued to graffiti the wall of the church.

"Hey," Jones repeated, grabbing the youth on the shoulder. "I'm talking to you."

This time, the boy turned around. "What?"

"What the hell do you think you're doing?"

The teenager shrugged and dropped the can into the flowerbed. Then, with a surprising lick of speed, he ran towards the old metal railings and vaulted over them before Jones had closed half of the distance between them.

"Get back here!"

The teenager just laughed and jogged away down the street. Jones put his foot on the railing and started to haul himself over, but the distance between them was already too great. Instead, he returned to the scene of the crime and inspected the damage. *Well*, he thought. *The kid has a point…*

It was there for the world to see, sprayed in metre-high letters on the wall of the holy church: 'THE END IS NIGH'.

Jones cursed to himself and picked up the aerosol from the flowerbed. He put it in his coat pocket and went to fetch the priest.

# CHAPTER THIRTY-FOUR: EXODUS

*Tuesday December 22nd, 2009*

**HIGH ABOVE** the cloud-line, the moon and stars shone brighter than ever before, undiluted by the dirt and the grime in the atmosphere. There was no sign of life – above was only space and desolation, mankind's final frontier. Way down below, occasional aircraft were invisible to the naked eye, tiny drops of life in the universe.

In the thin and unbreathable air, a storm was gathering. From every corner of the earth, from the nadir of the deep seas to the zenith of the highest mountains, the collective conscience of the Angels began to gather its forces and focus them on their terrible goal.

The stars blinked and went out, and the moon burned fiery white. At first, there was nothing but silence. Then, the terrible silhouettes of the Angels began to appear, an endless stream of naked light jetting forth from their celestial base of operations.

One by one, the Angels joined the formation like geese flying south for the winter. They grew steadily in number and took time to travel, allowing the army to expand into the night. A hundred thousand pricks of light pierced the darkness; the stars were back in the sky.

Several thousand kilometres away, the bright lights of the city signalled to the Angels in semaphore. They didn't speak;

they didn't have to. The terrible beings knew there was only one destination; they had a job to do, and no priest was going to get in their way.

# CHAPTER THIRTY-FIVE: COMEUPPANCE

*Wednesday December 23rd, 2009*

**JIMMY NEWCOMBE** prowled the streets with aerosols in his back pockets and a bag of chips breathing life into his frozen hands. His shift had been a busy one – when society starts breaking down, graffiti and vandalism spread like a malicious plague. Jimmy had a reputation to think of.

That's why he barely saw his parents, and why he'd spent two weeks' wages on paints and templates. New signatures, new logos, and new sentiments were springing up on walls and doors all over town, and Jimmy wasn't going to stand for it – these streets were his streets. He refused to be ousted by some punk with an attitude.

Jimmy jammed a final handful of chips into his mouth and threw the wrapper carelessly to the ground.

"You're going down," he muttered, spitting potato.

He reached into his back pocket, pulled out a blood-red aerosol, and began to spray his name onto the bins behind the curry house.

The deed done, he capped the aerosol and returned it to his pocket, then turned around to scan his surroundings for witnesses to the crime. He realised he wasn't alone – something stirred in the darkness at the end of the alleyway.

"Who's there?" he asked, receiving no response.

Suddenly, and with a brutal screech, a fox rocketed past him and into the busy street beyond, narrowly avoiding a head-on collision with a black SUV.

Jimmy watched it run and chuckled softly. "Damn it, why am I so jumpy?"

"Because you sensed that we were coming."

Jimmy clutched at his head as the beautiful choir hit him like an X-ray. He knew that voice – he'd heard it in his dreams, seen the creatures that it came from. Slowly, and bravely, he turned around.

"I know what you are," he said.

At first there were only two of them, but as the seconds passed, another half-dozen rose through the floor, always with the same impassive stare. When Jimmy turned around to scope his exit, it was blocked by a dozen more. Through the gaps in the phalanx, he saw cars pass along the road and away into the night. He felt alone.

"Then you know the purpose of our visit," they decreed. "Your help was most appreciated. The old priest will be saddened when he sees what you did to the walls of his precious church."

"I didn't do it for you," mumbled Jimmy.

"We know," they said. "But still, you have served your purpose and will be punished accordingly. You have lived a life of wasted opportunities and masochism. You have terrorised the neighbourhood at night and caused your parents the grief that they deserve. On the other hand, you have been helpful. We will give you an opportunity to speak."

"Can I speak with paint?"

The Angels seemed almost amused, though their expressions and their posture stayed ever-constant.

"I might not get another chance," Jimmy pleaded.

"Do as you please."

For the first time in his life, Jimmy signed a wall with his name, rather than his tag. The two pieces of graffiti shimmered in the light of the Angels. He paused for a second, stepped back to admire his handiwork, and then hurriedly sprayed a final word – 'Angels'.

Satisfied, he turned around to meet his antagonists. "I'm ready," he said.

The Angels were placated. "And so are we."

With their inscrutable faces and questionable sense of morality, they stepped forward and burned the artist, aerosols and all, and left his smoking corpse in the centre of the alley as a warning to the rest of humanity.

# CHAPTER THIRTY-SIX: THE LAST SUPPER

*Thursday December 24th, 2009*

**THEY ATE** in silence, the clink of cutlery echoing ominously through the chamber like chains around the ankles of a prisoner. The meal was tasteless but nourishing, a beef stew cooked on a portable stove.

Montgomery ate noiselessly with closed eyes, spooning the meaty broth between his papery gums. Jones slurped noisily and read the newspaper, dribbling stew onto every other page. It was full of the same bad news – lists of disappearances, the latest theories on the nature of the Angels, and, here and there, the occasional feel-good piece about the festive season. The former businessman sighed and put down his spoon.

"I can't take much more of this," he said.

Montgomery grunted and finished his meal by draining the liquid from the bowl.

"We have to do something. We're just sitting around and wasting time."

"I have a plan," replied Montgomery. "If we wait long enough, they'll come to us."

"And then what?"

"All in good time," Montgomery said. He sat serenely at the table, his eyes still shut tight against the influence of external stimuli. "Have patience."

"Uh-huh." Jones finished his meal and slid backwards on his chair.

As he stood up, the priest opened his eyes and took in Jones' flushed face and the pained look of exasperation that convoluted it.

"Sit down," Montgomery said. "Here, beside me."

Jones obeyed.

Montgomery continued, "There's something I need to tell you. I might not get another chance."

Jones said nothing – he just stared back at those wise old eyes.

"Do you remember what I told you about your mother?" Montgomery asked. "Your real mother? How she and I were close friends before her accident?"

"Of course," Jones replied. "How could I forget?"

"Quite. She made me promise to keep an eye on you, to make sure that you grew up to be a fine young man. I've done my best."

"You have." Jones looked almost bored.

Montgomery took his hands and stared at him. "But there's something I want you to know," he said. "It's time."

Jones smiled at the sudden role-reversal – he felt strengthened, empowered that just this once, he could be of help to the old man. "Confide in me, Father Montgomery."

"I…" he began. He stared morosely at his food, thought about what he was about to do, and lost confidence. Jones didn't need to hear the truth, not now. There'd be a time and a place for that, and it wasn't here and now.

"It's nothing," Montgomery said. "Just embrace me."

The two men rose and hugged. The priest shed a silent tear while Jones stood strong. For Montgomery, all of the evil in the world had disappeared – he was at peace, at last.

"Your mother would be so proud."

"Thanks, Father. It means a lot to hear you say that." The two men continued to hug in silence for a moment, and then Jones broke it off and patted him on the shoulder. "Come on, Father. We have a job to do."

Montgomery nodded, and they broke their embrace and left the rectory, walking through the dusty aisles and out into the night to meet the Angels.

# CHAPTER THIRTY-SEVEN: THE LAST STAND

*Thursday December 24th, 2009*

**THE STREETS WERE AWASH** with light, little beacons of hope in a desert of darkness, but that darkness was a sanctuary when faced with the awesome might of the Angels. No-one dared to leave their houses; they knew that the Angels were on the attack.

The streets were packed for kilometres around. An uncountable host of Angels had descended upon the city, united with a common goal, a common opponent. Jones and Montgomery stood arm-in-arm outside the church, facing the lines of light.

"Feel no fear," whispered the priest. "They feed on it and grow stronger."

"Who's afraid?" Jones' face betrayed him. "Let's do this."

Even Montgomery shook excitedly with the thrill of adrenaline.

Father and son walked to the boundary of the churchyard, noticing the little details – the yellow-green moss on the tombstones, the frozen tread of animal footprints in the holy soil, the condensation on the cars that lined the kerb outside the graveyard.

Outside the grounds, the Angels' leader stepped forward from his brethren and walked to meet Jones and Montgomery on the perimeter. The leader's beautiful, aquiline face was crippled with resentment, a deep-seated hatred for the good in the evil that surrounded him.

"Brothers," he howled, in a thunderous voice that sounded like the snapping of guitar strings. "Follow me to war."

"It's time," whispered Montgomery, steering Jones forward.

They met just outside the churchyard, and for the very first time, the two men realised the enormity of the task that they were facing. Of all of the thousands in front of them, not one of them was human.

Montgomery made the sign of the cross and held out a hand in greeting. The leader of the Angels laughed, a sound like the crackle of a blazing fire, and extended his own hand in return. They shook, and the stench and sound of burning flesh filled the air. Jones swallowed back vomit and tore his eyes away from Montgomery's withered arm; the priest didn't even react.

When Jones dared to look back at the two adversaries, the leader of the deadly host appeared astonished, if it were possible. Montgomery's right hand was a black mess of charred bone and singed skin, and the priest acted as if nothing were wrong.

"Let's begin," Montgomery said.

# CHAPTER THIRTY-EIGHT: EYES IN THE SKY

*Thursday December 24th, 2009*

**"ONE LAST LOOP,"** promised the co-pilot, trying to sooth the frayed nerves of his colleague. "You'll be back with the kids in no time."

"I won't. They're staying with their mother." Jonas, the pilot, sighed. "I won't see them this Christmas."

The helicopter circled slowly in the sky, scouring the streets for anything untoward. Patrol had been quiet tonight, unusually so. Crime rates were sky high thanks to the Angels. The superintendent had given in by now, and the officers were admitting that the perpetrators really were what they said they were – ghosts that could never be caught.

Jonas sighed again and prepared to turn back. "It's clean. Let's head home, it's Christmas Eve."

"Negative, sir." His co-pilot pointed at a dull glow on the horizon. "We're under orders, remember? We need to monitor the disturbance. Better check it out."

Jonas sighed for the third time, like the last breath of a dying man. The infernal glow of the Angels lit up the city and almost blinded them on their nearside. Something was afoot, but he didn't want to be the one to point it out.

The chopper veered left and coasted towards the fire. It shone like a beacon in the night, despite the light pollution.

The sight that awaited them was shocking. On the approach, the fire separated into thousands of tiny pinpricks shining like lanterns in the streets. It struck the moisture on the windshield and shone into the visors of the pilots, blinding them momentarily until Jonas had the good sense to veer right, leaving the Angels on the left.

"Oh my god," he breathed.

It was like something from another world; Hollywood effects on his doorstep. Only now could they take in the full enormity of what they were seeing – pavement after pavement, street after street, postcode after postcode of the gathered fury of the Angels, standing to attention and staring. The pilots could see dimly through polychromatic spheres that danced before their eyes. Jonas followed their gaze.

"Sweet Jesus," he said.

His friend and colleague looked like Jonas felt – terrified, and full of foreboding.

"There's a man down there."

# CHAPTER THIRTY-NINE: PARLEY

*Thursday December 24th, 2009*

**MONTGOMERY WAS SWEATING** like an animal, but his eyes were as stolid as always. He stood proud beside his son, examining the remains of his hand in the Angel-light.

"I must meet their leader as an equal," said Montgomery, answering Jones' unspoken question. "It's the only way."

The Angels laughed as one, then their leader spoke. "You are quite right, old man. This is the only way it can be. Your child may leave us."

"I'm not a child," Jones growled.

"But you once were. Did your father never tell you about your true parentage? The man that you stand beside is the man whose sin impregnated your mother. You, my child, are born of sin. We will take great pleasure in destroying you."

Jones was stunned – he looked into the priest's eyes, and saw the truth, at last. His heart rose and sank at the same time, filled with renewed love for his father and renewed hatred for his adversary. Montgomery squeezed his hand and stepped forward.

"He will stay right here, beside me. You and I are not so dissimilar. But I see the best in people, and you see the worst."

The Angel nodded. "Agreed. The worst is so much more… nourishing."

The three syllables could've shattered glass. Jones just stood there and watched – he knew he was insignificant beside his father and the Angel, the leader of men and the leader of everything men feared.

"And you're agreed we're at a stalemate?" Montgomery asked.

"We could just kill you. But I am interested in you, little man. You have sins that no-one else can offer us, and your position makes you unique among the vermin you share the planet with."

Montgomery smiled, sadly. "You know all about me, but I know nothing about you. Grant me the privilege of knowing who I'm facing."

"I have nothing to tell," growled the leader of the Angels. "I exist because of the evil in others. I have found myself, taken shape, and grown because of you and the rest of your kind."

"Where did you come from?" Montgomery asked.

"Your scientists brought us forth. They were trying to disprove God."

"And is there a God?" he pressed.

"There is only us," the Angel replied.

They watched each other for a minute or so, standing in uneasy silence. Montgomery closed his eyes and prepared himself.

Finally, he spoke. "There's only one way out of this. We must switch our views and experience each other's perspective. You must see the world like a priest, and I must see it like an Angel."

The leader thought with the combined brain of an entire army. Every soul they'd ever swallowed, every deed they'd done, and every piece of depravity and sin they'd ever witnessed converged into one resentful whole.

The Angels decided – they would be open-minded. They would see the world through the priest's eyes. The evil leader looked the priest in the eye and sealed the infernal deal.

"We will do it."

# CHAPTER FORTY: SACRIFICE

*Thursday December 24th, 2009*

**MONTGOMERY WAS ON FIRE.** His entire being repulsed him; he was held together by spit and dust, sin, lies, and bodily fluids. The world was multi-faceted, filled with colours he didn't know the name of.

Jones stood beside him, the living incarnation of his own evil doings. Somewhere, dead and buried in the grounds of a run-down church, Sarah at least was unpunished – she was never touched by Angels.

Everything, everywhere, stirred a deep hatred within him. He could never un-see what he was seeing, he could never be Montgomery again. He looked through the haze at his opponent, whose sole ambition he started to understand, and at his son who stood still beside him, finally aware of the carnal sin that planted seed in Sarah's stomach.

The hatred began to build – of himself, of his fellow man, and of his son. The Angels' eyes lit up with comprehension. Montgomery stared down at the twisted mortal hand that lay useless by his side. That pain was nothing compared to the evil that boiled his blood and wracked his brain in useless spasms. The defeated priest fell to the floor in subservience.

\* \* \*

They saw it now – they saw it all, everything the priest had told them about goodness and humanity. The stars above them were beautiful, a twinkling mirror image of the massed ranks of the murderous, unstoppable, avenging Angels.

They saw it all. How they'd sentenced Angelica to death, how they'd judged as inadequate every other life-form that had crossed their path. For a brief second, every Angel experienced the same emotion – a profound and disturbing regret.

This was something unforgettable. Even their leader, the first Angel to come forth into this new universe, was changed forever. They felt the wind in the trees, the light patter of snow that fizzled and melted on their flesh, cooling their angry bodies.

In one last, desperate movement, their leader stepped forward and touched the cowering priest on the forehead, burning the mark of the Angels into his skull. The old man dropped to the floor, dead.

*   *   *

The shriek of the grieving Angels tore the sky in two, wiping out power lines and deafening the vermin that scattered down alleyways away from them. They'd never felt this pain, this sheer remorse at a terrible act that, once done, could not be undone.

As one, they turned upon their leader and descended upon him with sharp, sinister teeth and talons that sprouted from their warped, demonic bodies. He wailed in mortal fear, seeing the end in their flashing eyes. Then he was gone, torn apart and scattered in the gutters.

Ashamed of their depravity and now leaderless, the Angels covered their genitalia with fleshy hands and disappeared into the night. They resolved to see the good in everything, to see it as they saw it now – omnipresent and all consuming.

*   *   *

Jones crumpled as the Angels closed ranks, the heat and horror of it all too much for him to bear; on his knees, through tear-filled eyes, he could see their embarrassed faces. Inhumanly perfect, but just as flawed by sin. For a moment, he thought he saw Montgomery rise towards the heavens; then he passed out, the last person ever to lay eyes on the priest.

A shrill siren screamed through the air, and the police helicopter lit up the sky with powerful flashlights. It was seven minutes before the first officer arrived on the scene. There was no sign of any disturbance, just a comatose man in a dusty suit, spattered with burned blood and coated in his own vomit. No Angels meant no disturbance, and no disturbance meant their last shift of the day was over.

They took him to the drunk tank and went home to spend Christmas with their families.

# CHAPTER FORTY-ONE: JONES' CLOSURE

*Friday January 1st, 2010*

**I WELCOMED** the New Year on a hospital bed, sleeping in fits and dreaming of darkness and despair. Medically, there was nothing wrong with me, but consciousness was a struggle. I felt half-dead, on the verge between good and evil, and my eyes had been opened forever.

So, the priest was my father – perhaps I should've known. I loved him, and I knew that he loved me. I saw it in his eyes at the end, and I understood. I hope that wherever he is, he's waiting for me in the afterlife, with the angels. He saved us all, and he solved the unsolvable. The doctors tell me he's dead, but I'm not so sure. My father, he's a martyr, and no-one knows his name.

Perhaps unsurprisingly, the police don't believe a word of it – they just think I'm crazy. I don't care, because the Angels are gone for good. The newspapers are in uproar, they have nothing else to write about. Reality is slowly returning. Perhaps this way, the whole ugly episode can be forgotten.

But my father will always be remembered in the hearts of the people that he helped when they had nowhere else to turn, by the drunks and the addicts that sheltered in the rectory, and by me, his only son. Goodbye, father.

**THE END**

# ACKNOWLEDGMENTS

Where do you start with something like this? First off, big thanks to Jesse James Freeman and the management team at Booktrope for helping me to chase the dream, one book at a time.

If you enjoyed NO REST FOR THE WICKED, it's because of the tireless work put in by my team – Laura Bartha (the best editor I've ever worked with), Ashley Ruggirello (cover artist extraordinaire), and Jennifer Farwell (my long-suffering proofreader).

Thanks also go to my family, for putting up with my erratic behaviour – Donna Woodings, Heather and Dave Clarke, and Alan and Olga Woodings in particular.

If you want to achieve greatness, you need to surround yourself with people who are doing great things. Big thanks to Allie Burke, Rosy Illustrates, Michael-Israel Jarvis, Ant and Ali Lightfoot, Alex Nimier, Imran Siddiq, Matt Sears, and Maddie Von Stark for doing great things on a daily basis and keeping me inspired when it's three o'clock in the morning and I have a deadline to make.

And the most heartfelt thanks of all go to you, the reader. Stay awesome.

# JOIN THE CONVERSATION

Well, you made it this far – congratulations on avoiding the Angels!

Whether you loved the book or you hated it, I want to know what you think – join the conversation by tweeting @DaneCobain or using the #Booktrope hashtag.

danecobain.com

twitter.com/danecobain

facebook.com/danecobainmusic

# MORE GREAT READS
# FROM BOOKTROPE

*Phobia* **by Daniel Lance Wright** (Thriller) Heights, crowds, small spaces... How does a psychologist handle three phobia sufferers on a cruise ship in the Gulf of Mexico when the ship is overtaken by Lebanese terrorists?

*Rachel's Folly* **by Monica Bruno** (Thriller) Told from three unique perspectives, RACHEL'S FOLLY is a thrilling exploration of profound loss, morality, and the lengths to which we will go to keep our darkest secrets.

*Skull Dance* **by Gerd Balke and Michael Larocca** (Thriller) An atmospheric tale of international nuclear espionage, intrigue and heroism, twisted politics, terrorism, and romance.

*The Key to Everything* **by Alex Kimmell** (Thriller) When Auden discovers a curious leather-bound book, its contents will soon endanger his entire family. The pages of this book draw him into a prison that cannot be breached, a place that can only be unlocked with a very special key.

Discover more books and learn about our
new approach to publishing at **booktrope.com**.

Lightning Source UK Ltd.
Milton Keynes UK
UKOW04f0805011215

263872UK00002B/30/P